Three On The Planet Arena

D1743736

Daisy Kight Chandler

Pen Press Publishers Ltd
London

Published in the Great Britain by
Pen Press Publishers Ltd,
39-41 North Road,
Islington,
London N7 9DP

ISBN 1 900796 23 6

Cover Design by Bridget Tyldsley

About The Author

Daisy Kight Chandler was born in 1932 in Lambeth Walk, London.

She joined the WRAF in 1949 and became a police dog handler, starting the Aveley Dog Training Club fifteen years later.

She is now an Honorary Member and President of the Aveley Obedience and Working Trials Society Dog Club.

Besides dogs, particularly German Shepherds, Daisy loves gardening.

With Vena, her beloved Alsatian

She also plays and composes music for the organ, and writes poetry. She now lives in Tilbury, Essex.

This is the third book in the Planet Arena trilogy.

CHAPTER ONE
THE AWAKENING

I had rested well and felt I wanted to see my world again. I felt extremely fit except for the weight of my body and limbs, which felt like lead, and I was unable to move them. I had the feeling of being held back; this caused a little anger in me. The urge to shout at my captors was strong, but an uncanny sense of fear prevented me from doing this. I felt the restraints being taken from my wrists and a pressure lifted from my eyes.

'Come along now, you are awake.'

I knew that voice, but I couldn't put a name to it. Opening my eyes to that dimly lit room made me think of the Dwellers and I gasped.

'It is all right, my dear, you are with friends.'

Looking at the man beside me I smiled and whispered, 'Minu.'

'Of course, child, who did you expect?'

'I don't know, it's been a long time.'

'Do you feel rested, dear?'

'Yes thank you, sir, very much better. I cannot remember what happened.'

'You had two beautiful children, my dear, but it proved too much for you. You have been reborn to Claire. You must be patient with each other until you become one.'

'I love life, I do so want to live it again.'

'I was hoping to hear you say that. You are a good girl.'

I ran my fingers through my hair and saw it was brown.

'My hair, Minu, it has gone!'

I felt very disappointed at that; I was proud of my beautiful long Saxon hair. I touched my face and asked if I might rise from my bed. Inca and Amnia helped me to my feet, but I didn't find it very easy, so they walked me to and fro until I was more confident.

1

By this time the lights had been brought back to strength so I took stock of my surroundings. There was another woman present who I knew as Ekka, Claire's guardian. She smiled pleasingly at me and I could not help but return the compliment, for I had a great liking for her. But as nice as everyone was, I couldn't help feeling there was something missing, and to top it all there was a terrible fear within me, something that suppressed me.

'Can I look in the mirror, Minu?'

Inca led me to the looking glass and it would be true to say I was shocked to see such a young girl of only eighteen years old, not unattractive, but so innocent-looking and afraid.

'Claire,' I whispered as I reached out and touched my image. I felt so sad for her as I felt her fear. I, Jan, was afraid. Jan, I thought, or am I Claire?

'Who are you?' asked Minu softly.

'Yes, who am I? An image?' I whispered. 'I do not know. Claire, I think.'

Minu touched my arm and I drew away from him saying, 'You are not my uncle.'

'No, Claire, the days of uncles are behind you, dear. That was a long time ago. We are Arenians, do you remember?'

'Yes, sir,' I replied, wishing him to keep his distance.

'You are not still afraid of me, are you, Claire?'

I stared at him thinking: this is a man I have always liked and trusted, yet I fear him.

'Claire?' he said again.

'I want to go home,' I told him with a little cry in my voice, 'I want to go home.'

He turned to Ekka and told her, 'I do not wish the child to be distressed. Take her home now and I will contact you when she has settled.'

Ekka offered me her hand and led me to the door. As it swished open, I turned, feeling I had forgotten something, but there was nothing in that room that held anything for me, so I turned to Ekka, who took me home.

I had asked Ekka to take me home, but once she had done

so, it was only a place I had seen. It did not have the feeling of home. I knew my way around the apartment; I knew which room was mine, but it was quite alien to me. Looking towards the garden I asked, "Where are my trees?'

'Trees?' repeated Ekka. 'You never had trees, Claire.'

Claire, of course not, but I'm not Claire. I turned to Ekka with anger for bringing me to the wrong home, but as I looked at her I felt my courage drain and I found myself retreating from her, and a horrifying feeling at having thought badly of her.

'I'm sorry, Ekka,' I whimpered.

She smiled reassuringly at me and said, 'There is nothing to be sorry for, Claire. Now settle down, dear, and I will bring us refreshments.'

By the Mother, they have given me a cringing coward for a shell, too gutless to say my name! I'm imprisoned!

Ekka had switched the vision viewer on for me and I sat watching it, almost afraid to look elsewhere, but I was not in the least bit interested in it. Suddenly the door burst open and a young Arenian entered.

'Fern!' I shrieked with delight as I ran to greet her. 'Fern, I had forgotten you!'

I held her hand and pulled her joyfully into the room. She looked over my shoulder and said, 'Hello Ekka', then looking at me she asked, 'How are you today, Claire?'

Before I could answer, Ekka told Fern to tidy herself up while she got her tea. I released my grip on Fern as she went towards her room. Like a little lamb I followed her, and on reaching her door I halted, knowing instinctively that it was forbidden to cross it without being invited to do so.

Fern turned to me, patted the foot of her bed and whispered, 'Come in, Claire.'

I sat on the foot of the bed while Fern showered and changed behind me.

'Was today a good day for you, Claire?'

'I'm not sure,' I told her.

'Why is that?'

3

'I got lost, Fern.'

'Lost, where?'

'I don't know.'

There was silence for what seemed an age as I tried to sort out my thoughts and remember things. I remembered Fern well enough when she came in: she is my Arenian house sister and she shares everything with me. No one could have a nicer sister, even though she is seven years older than me.

Suddenly she put her arm around my shoulder as I rose and we left her room.

As we approached the table, Fern asked, 'Where was Claire when you found her, Ekka?'

Ekka stared at us both and replied, 'What are you talking about, girl?'

'Claire said she got lost today.'

'No, Fern, you don't understand,' I pleaded with her.

Fern looked at me questioningly as Ekka said, 'What exactly did you say, Claire?'

I sidled up to Fern and said sheepishly, 'I told Fern I got lost.'

'Now why did you lie? You have never lied before, Claire,' said Ekka.

'I didn't, Ekka, I just meant I'm lost inside.'

Ekka's eyes melted and she said, 'I can understand that, child, it is very apparent from your speech. After dinner this evening, I want you to write all that you have felt today in your log-book. Is that clear, my dear?'

'Yes, ma'am,' I replied without question.

'One of you will materialize eventually,' she said, seating herself at the table. 'Now sit and drink your tea.'

Two days passed and Ekka thought that I would be better employed back at my schooling than moping about the apartment, so off to school it was.

There were eight Earthians, all my age, in the class tutored by Isha, whom we addressed as Ma'am. She had always been a very pleasant and fair Arenian and I liked her.

On that first day back, she treated me as though I had never been away, which made me feel more at ease. I became embarrassed very easily, not a bit like my old self. If only I could break through this web of fear.

'Our first lesson today will be geography. Elizabeth, be kind enough to see that each young lady has an atlas book.'

Elizabeth placed the book before me, and I seemed to be mesmerised by it. I clasped it to me as though afraid someone might steal it. Somehow that book of maps seemed so important to me.

'Turn to page five,' Isha told us.

I fumbled, all fingers and thumbs. Page five was forgotten as I turned the pages, searching.

People were talking but I didn't listen; I had to find it. Why hadn't I seen this book before? A hand spread across the book, stopping the pages turning. I pushed it but it was too strong and a voice said aloud, 'Claire, what is the matter, child?'

I froze with fear. It was Isha, and she held my map hard to the table.

'Are you unwell, my dear?'

She looked very kind and gentle, but her hand never moved from the map, and I wouldn't dare answer her. I stared at the book and slowly she took her hand away until I could hold the book again.

'Do you want the book, Claire?'

I looked up at her and nodded.

'Very well, dear, you may keep it.'

That was very kind. I think I like her even more now.

Isha sat at her desk and I sat at mine. The other Earthians were gone. That was the part I couldn't understand: I never saw them leave.

'Shall we talk about your book, Claire?'

'It's just another lesson to Claire. I want the book, me, Jan.'

'Now I understand, Jan. Claire is hindering you.'

'She is one hell of a wally, she is afraid of everything, she annoys me.'

'You must be patient, Jan. Claire is very young.'

'She is too Earth-like for me. Arenians aren't afraid.'

5

'But Jan is an Earthling.'

'No, Jan's an Arenian. Jan was a trooper and killed Earthians. Earth people don't like Arenians, did you know that, Isha?'

Isha just smiled and said, 'Why do you want the book, Jan?'

'They spoilt my Earth, Isha, I want to see if my England is still there.'

'You just told me you were Arenian, Jan, yet now you speak of your Earth world.'

I looked at her and thought: you are so clever and yet you cannot see I can still love the things that were once mine. I looked down at the book and moved my hand across it in a stroke-like movement and said, 'I still have memories, they will always be mine.'

'Welcome,' said Isha, and I shot a glance at her, then to the door. It was Minu.

'Who have we here?' he asked with interest as he walked to Isha's side.

'Claire came to class, but it would seem we now have Jan.'

'It was to be expected,' Minu stated. 'Well, Jan, what have you to say for yourself?' he said as he tilted his head to one side and observed me.

I looked him straight in the eyes and told him, 'You should be ashamed of yourself, sir, giving a child an adult's task, and such a cowardly girl she is.'

He straightened his shoulders as though ready to do battle with me and said, 'I will not have you call Claire cowardly. She is very young and has endured great hardship. If you had taken the time to study her log-book, then perhaps you would find a little compassion for your fellow being.'

'How the hell can I, if she is afraid of everything about her and she didn't give me a chance to gather my thoughts?' I shouted at him.

'Then what better place than a classroom to inform you of the child you bear such ill-will towards. For a start, Jan, Claire did not have her full course of therapy with you. Unfortunately you were too weak and your brain suffered a relapse. Thanks

6

be to our Mother, you made the transition in time. I regret to say you died, my dear, rather prematurely. Now perhaps you can see why you have been hindered in this way. Let me tell you about Claire, and try to mould you into one. After all, you need each other if you are to survive.'

He proceeded to tell me of 'little Claire', as he referred to her with affection. Apparently Claire was born in 1932, to a middle class family. She had an older brother who was inclined to spoil her; he was five years older than she and was quite the little protector with her. She would trot behind him like a well-trained puppy, sometimes to his annoyance. He was always called Edward by his parents, but this was too much of a mouthful for one so young so she shortened it to suit her vocabulary and always called him Eddie.

As Minu told me of Claire, so I relived her memories. I could see it all as though it were yesterday. 'Wait for me, Eddie!' she would call, and very reluctantly yet patiently he would slow his pace for her to catch up. Then she would slide her hand into his and, looking aloft to him, she would ask where they were going. Not that she cared, as long as her Eddie was with her.

In 1939 war broke out and their father insisted that Claire and Edward went to the country for safety. With what seemed a hundred or more children, they were labelled and bundled on boats and coaches to the secluded parts of the country far away from the towns.

Claire was seven years old by now and although she was dwarfed by her brother she began to treat him like her dolls, telling him not to get too close to the rails of the boat for fear of him falling into the water. They had been given packs of sandwiches to sustain them on their day's journey and she reminded him that Mummy had told them to wash their hands before eating. To shut her up he wiped her hands on a clean handkerchief and she settled for second best. He watched her eat and felt sad as he saw her eyes scanning the other children and noticed her sidle closer to him. As he put a brotherly arm about her shoulder she rested her head on his chest and complained to him that she missed Mummy, then she cried herself to sleep as he buttoned her coat to keep her warm. He was all she had at that terrible parting from her mother, and although Mother she tried to be, she needed Eddie's protection much more.

It was as though I was outside myself, being told of major incidents in Claire's life and surveying them from a vantage point, but I could feel all her pain.

Claire and Edward arrived at the little Suffolk village only to find they had to be separated. Claire was to go to a lady she was to call Auntie Rose and her brother a mile away to another family.

That night was one of the worst nights she had experienced, the first night parted from every member of her family: cold, alone, and with an ache in her tummy that she knew would only go away when her mother put her arms around her.

Many times that night she awoke in the darkness and whimpered, glad of the dawn and the hope of seeing her Eddie. He would put all to rights.

By the time she was nine years old, she learned one day when her mother visited her that Eddie was being taken home to start work. He was grown up and could earn a wage, plus care for his mother while their father soldiered at war. Life without her brother would be unbearable and she clung to her mother on that day, dreading the setting of the sun when she knew her world would disappear. That had been a tearful time and even Eddie had found it hard to keep a stiff upper lip. Auntie Rose had made a special high tea for her, but because of her crying she had been sick and could keep nothing down.

From that day on, Claire was permitted to stay up a little later in the evenings. She was permitted to meet all Auntie Rose's relatives and she was told to call them Uncle. Sleep came easier after the excitement of meeting the uncles, who would tease her and bring her those rare commodities, chocolate and chewing gum.

Six months later her mother and Eddie visited her again and she told Eddie how nice he looked in his black suit and black tie, but asked him why he had a black silk ribbon round the top of his arm. He told her it was a special mark of respect that grown-ups wear, so she didn't question him further, but she did notice her mother was wearing a black diamond sewn on her sleeve. Claire didn't feel quite so bad this time when they left for home. Mummy had told her the war would soon be over and they would be together again, and her Eddie treated her more like a dad than a brother.

That was the last time she ever saw them. I could not control Claire's tears as she wept freely in front of Minu and Isha. Minu offered me a clean handkerchief and Isha brought me a glass of water as I tried to restrain my sobs. Then Minu continued.

Three weeks later a man and a woman came to see Auntie Rose. They had asked Claire to show them the room she slept in, asked was she happy there and what she had for dinner. When they left, Auntie Rose seemed to treat her differently. She was given chores to do when she got home from school, and she had to help entertain the uncles while Auntie Rose made herself look pretty.

The days grew longer and she wished many times that her mother and Eddie would come and take her home again, but it was not to be. Only the uncles visited.

One uncle in particular, a sailor that Aunt Rose called Wilf, stayed for a whole week, and Claire had grown to dislike him.

At first it seemed like a game when he tickled her and let her drink beer from his glass, only to see her pull a face at the horrible taste. But one day he ran his hands over her chest and told Aunt Rose she would be as bonnie as her one day.

Aunt Rose had grown cross and told him never to touch the child again or he would not be welcome. Then, taking her anger out on Claire, she slapped her and told her to get into the kitchen and get the tea things washed.

Looking back now, she could understand Aunt Rose's anger and cringed.

Minu continued to talk as though from a long way off, as Claire's thoughts drifted through time and remembered Uncle

Hank the American airman who had told her all about the ranch he owned in Texas and how he was great pals with all the film star cowboys of that time. Claire had been very impressed with it all and readily believed him when he gave her a whole bar of chocolate and a bottle of soda-pop while he and Aunt Rose went out for the evening.

By the time she was eleven years old, Claire was practically running Aunt Rose's house, and it had got to the stage where Aunt Rose was asking Claire what she thought she should wear that evening and where she could find the clean clothes. Claire would bring them from the pile of ironing and place the garments over a chair for her, telling Aunt Rose she would be in bed with her door locked by the time she got home. She hadn't forgotten the night Aunt Rose came home legless and had passed out, only to leave an amorous soldier trying to force his way into Claire's room. She had put the back of the chair under the handle of the door in fear that the lock would give way, and she did it every night after that, so Auntie never tried her door after she had retired. Claire would open it to no one.

The night was clear, the moon was full and every star in the heavens glowed. It was two am and Auntie was still not home. If Claire had fallen asleep earlier, this worry for Aunt Rose would not have prevailed, but alas the late hour had her very concerned for Auntie's well-being. She got dressed and made herself a warm drink, as the fire was out and there was a cold chill in the air. Twice she walked to the front gate and peered along the lane, but there was nothing, not even a hoot of an owl. She poked the dead embers in the grate but they were cold, so she replenished her cup, put her coat round her shoulders and stood at the gate. The stars were like jewels set on black velvet and the moon like another world made of pearl.

It was at this time she caught sight of a man coming towards her. She raised her arm and asked if he had passed a blonde-haired lady. He assured her that if he had he would have asked her where the road was that led to the other side of the woods.

'Are you an American?' she asked.

'Why?' he said smiling.

'You look like one, they wear funny clothes like you.'

'No, I am not American, I am Arenian. Do you know where the road is by the woods?'

'Where is Arena?' she asked.

'That is a secret,' he told her.

'I bet that's in America. Americans are always saying things are secret if they don't want to talk about them, and you're not from hereabouts or you would know that's a spinney.'

Suddenly Claire moved back a pace and whispered, 'You're not a bloody German are you?'

Seeing her fear he laughed heartily and said, 'I should hope not.'

She smiled and leaned back on the gate. 'I bet you are cold, mister. I can't ask you in, but you are welcome to some of my tea.'

'You are most kind, but I must find the road past the woods,' he told her.

'You won't find it at night, mister, it's not a road, just a foot-path.'

'Then I am lost,' he said looking about him, 'utterly lost.'

'Hold on, mister, I won't see you lost.' And Claire placed her cup on the gate-post and joined the Arenian in the lane.

'Come on, Yank, I'll put you on the right path. After all, we are on the same side, eh?'

He grinned at her, telling her to button her coat against the cold night air. She buttoned her coat, telling him her cup of tea would keep the cold out.

They followed the path that ran beside the spinney as she told him to watch his footing for clumped grass and bracken till there, before her, reflecting the moonlight, was a silver dome. She froze in her tracks and stared in wonder. The stranger's voice broke the silence as he said, 'You have indeed been a friend, I shall repay my debt to you, child.' And as he gripped her arm she spun round to meet his eyes that burned into her mind.

'Since that time she has lived and been schooled as an

11

Arenian. Now you are Jan or Claire, which ever one you choose to be, my child.'

I raised my face from my hands and mopped the tears away.

'Well, Jan, or is it Claire?' he asked.

'Jan,' I whispered. 'What happened to her mother and brother?'

'They died in the war, but although Claire never asked, I think she knew,' Minu replied, quite concerned.

'She was afraid of the truth because it hurts,' I told him.

He walked towards me and rested his hand on my head, saying, 'There will always be some pain in life, but now you have each other the pain will not be so great. Have faith in Arena, and perhaps there will be no pain at all.'

'I am Arenian and this is my home, Minu.'

'May our Mother always smile on you, child, you please me greatly,' he said with pleasure.

Then he turned to Isha and bade her open the door. Her hand went to her belt-activator and the door swished open. To my delight Jena entered, nodded her respects to Minu and Isha. Then she stood looking at me. I pushed Minu aside and ran to her. 'Mum, it's my mum!' I cried as I hugged her.

She made no move to greet me. She stood silent, still looking at Minu.

'She is your responsibility now, Jena,' said Minu.

Jena looked down at me and smiled. Only then did I feel safe in the arms of my mum and friend.

'Take her home, Jena, she needs you and the security that only you can give her.'

Jena nodded her thanks to Minu and Isha, then we left the school room, I hoped for the last time.

Chapter Two
The Acceptance

Oh to be back home to that familiar warmth that only one's own home has! Jena said very little to me except to answer me, and I wondered if I had upset her.

'Aren't we friends any longer, Jena?'

She only smiled and brought me a cup of tea.

'Don't you like me as Claire?'

'Claire is very young, Jan, you must be gentle with her. You have left her with a mammoth task. It is not going to be easy for any of us, least of all Claire.'

We observed each other until I had to look away, and I said as casually as I could muster, 'Why do you side with Claire? She will never love you as much as I do.'

'Oh we most certainly have Jan here, but for how long? You do not realize, Jan, that Claire could not possibly make the full transition in the time she was with you. She needed at least another six months, but you died, Jan, and I fear now that we may lose each other if you do not follow my advice.'

I turned and grinned at her. 'Jena, you worry too much. I have no intention of leaving and letting this eighteen-year-old, pale-faced pip-squeak take my place.'

'I am pleased to hear it, Jan, and no doubt you will be pleased to hear that you will study your log-book for five hours each day to ensure that does not happen.'

'By the Power, Jena, I shall have no time to spend with Karl. It's not fair!'

'Fair or not, that is what you will do. Claire is far too young to mate.'

'You are wicked, Jena. To think that someone you love could be so cruel! You are inhuman.'

Jena laughed and took my cup, leaving me pondering over

what she had said. I didn't know how long it had been since I had seen Karl, but if she thought I could study with Karl on my mind, then she was sorely wrong.

For two weeks I studied my log-book, and at times I cried as I relived my memories. It really hurt me when I read of Delt being killed. He was a wonderful man, a terrible loss to Arena and our troop. Then of course there was the time Virg rejected my advances. How stupid could I have been to think a non-productive Arenian would have given me a second glance! I was stupid. I suppose I shall have to meet the Dwellers and be familiarized with them once again. My old Karshaa will be dead now, and I shall have to tread with care when I meet his rival. Oh Mother of Arena, how long before I can meet my Karl? Jena is good and kind, but Karl is my greatest love.

I wandered from my room to my garden, and hugged the big oak tree. Oh to be as strong and wise as the oak, I thought. Then I remembered it was but a fake, so I turned my back to it and used it to lean upon. What is real? I wondered. am I Claire or Jan? I must be Jan inside Claire's frame, for I yearn so for Karl.

'Jena,' I called, and in no time at all she was beside me. 'Jena, who am I?' I asked in panic.

'Only you can answer that, Jan.'

'I know what I feel, Jena, but I am uncertain when I look into the mirror.'

'My dear child, that is quite understandable. You are young, time is young, do not try to run before you can walk,' she told me, smiling at my dilemma.

'When can I see Karl?'

'I have told you, child, you are too young for coupling. Now put it out of your mind.'

'But if I could just see him?'

'Jan, you have said many times, to see him is to want him. Why do you Earthlings torture yourselves so?'

I hung my head in shame, knowing she knew my innermost thoughts, and I whispered, 'I love him.'

I glanced up and saw the pity she had for me in her eyes and she said, 'I shall see what can be done about the matter.'

14

I knew then that if it was at all possible for me to see Karl, then Jena would be as good as her word. Now I waited and prayed.

Two days later, Jena told me Karl would be coming to dinner on the condition I knew how to conduct myself. Bloody cheek, I thought, and I his wife!

The moment arrived as the door swished open and my beautiful Arenian husband stood in the doorway like a Greek god of love. We stood in silence for a few breathless seconds, then he ventured to approach me. Only then did I realize Claire's fear, as I felt the blood drain from me and an ice cold fear gripped me.

Karl slowed his pace as I backed away with every step he took. He halted, his smile gone and replaced with a questioning stare.

Jena's hand slid into mine as she led me to a chair. By Jesus and our Mother, here was the man I had been yearning for, and this stupid little bitch Claire was denying him. What the bloody hell am I going to do with her? I'm hungry for him.

'Is she sick, Jena?' asked Karl.

'Claire has come forth, Karl. You have familiarized yourself with her history, I hope?'

'Yes indeed,' replied Karl as he moved to the other side of the room and sat down.

Here they were, discussing me as though I was not present, although I must confess, it was as though I was locked in a time capsule and unable to break free.

'Perhaps it would be prudent for you to leave, Karl,' requested Jena. Karl rose from his chair as I cringed, and he left us. As the door shut behind him, I sprang from my chair and called him, but he was gone. I felt a terrible sinking feeling within the pit of my stomach, and a pain in my throat as I tried to suppress the tears. Slamming my fist on the table I screamed, 'What have they done to me? I'm no longer Jan, I am two people. In the name of Holiness, what have you done to me, Jena?'

'Time has never been kind to you, Jan, this is your chance to make it work for you. Give yourself time, child.'

15

'Time, always time,' I whispered as I rested my head in my hands and wept. 'I hate all Arenians, I hate you for what you are doing to me. Time and Earthians are just something you amuse yourselves with, and I won't play your game.'

'Life is not a game, as you will see as it passes and you grow up, Jan.'

'I don't want any part of your world, it hurts me too much. I am a woman in a child's frame. You have cheated me.'

She tried to comfort me but I rebuffed her good intentions by mimicking her talk of time being my friend.

'Sarcasm does not become you, Jan, but if that is the only way you can contain your temper, then you may proceed, but only as long as I permit it.'

'Sod it,' I muttered under my breath, and I went to my room.

I flicked idly through my log-book and Copper's name took my eye. I returned to Jena, log-book in hand and asked if she knew what had become of Copper and Robert. She told me she knew nothing for certain, only hearsay. Robert had deserted when a trooper and Copper had been recalled for breeding. She had not made it her business to keep informed.

'Oh, I thought you knew everything, Jena.'

'Well, my dear, now you know I do not.'

I looked at my log and said, 'There is a lot of reading here.'

'The written word imprints itself in one's memory. It is better that you read it yourself.'

I looked pained at her, but she only smiled at me and shook her head as she retired to her glass cubicle.

'I love you, Mum,' I called.

'I know,' was her distant reply.

I sat and read my log-book.

I arose the following morning and sat down to breakfast with Jena. I told her I had dreamed in the night and thought it strange knowing my brain had died but the dream was mine and not Claire's.

'That is quite natural since you read Jan's log-book yesterday.'

'I dreamed of my home on Earth. Sitting by the fireside and

16

talking to Jim. I could see his smile and feel the warmth, comfort and contentment. It was nice, almost beautiful. I was sorry it had to end.'

She made no comment.

'Do you dream Jena?'

'Only by design.'

'That's silly. You can't choose dreams.'

'I can with my imagery machine.'

'Your what?'

'I can put on the imagery headpiece, turn it to record while reading or listening to my log-book, and record my visions. It will play them back to me on request.'

'By our Mother, that's clever, Jena! Can I do that?'

'You will one day.'

'Self-made movies from thought. Aren't Arenians clever?'

'We have had a few hundred years longer on this planet to perfect such things, Jan.'

'When can I have some of these things to play with?'

'That is the trouble, Jan, everything is a game and nothing is cherished and respected.'

'Chance would be a fine thing. I'm not afraid of robots any more.'

'Any longer,' she corrected me.

'Well, whatever. So why can't I have one to talk to?And if I had a dream machine, I could learn my log-book twice as fast.'

She looked at me distastefully, shook her head, finished eating and cleared the table. I watched her out the corner of my eye for a sign to push my luck further, but it wasn't forthcoming.

By late afternoon she called me from my garden and pointed to my room.

'I haven't done anything,' I said in self-defence.

'The robot you requested has just arrived. It is in your room.'

I rushed in, thinking I was going to find a huge parcel to unwrap. Imagine my surprise to see a tin box the size of a biscuit tin on my writing desk.

'It's a box,' I proclaimed, feeling cheated.

'It is one of the early models of talking computer robots. If you can treat it with the respect we were discussing this morning, then I shall try to get you a better one. That was all I could get at such short notice. Press the switch at the side and talk to it. You will be surprised how much it can teach you. Now I must return to my console.' And she left me looking at the sad little tin box that was going to teach me so much. Where's the wire to plug it in? I wondered. No wires; it must have a battery in it, although I couldn't see where it might be located. Well, now for it. So I flicked the switch and said, 'Hi, I'm Jan, good afternoon, what's your name?'

I waited, and waited, and got fed up waiting. So I tapped it on the top with my knuckles and said louder, 'Oi, are you at home?'

'*Home*,' said a metallic voice as I made a quick exit to the door and waited as I gathered my dignity.

'Home,' I called back, to let it know I welcomed it.

The metallic voice answered. 'Home. A dwelling place. Birth place. A place to be familiar. Available to family. End of marathon. An achievement. A missile guiding beam ...'

'Shut up ... Stop ... Bloody thing.' And I flicked the switch.

Dear God and little fishes, it's a dictionary, a bloody dictionary! How does she think I'm going to learn from it if I can't talk with it?

I stood looking at the damn thing and flicked the switch again. Nothing happened so I up and downed the switch a few times. 'Got nothing to say now have you? Cat got your tongue?' I said to it as I gave it another bang on the top.

'Tongue. A muscular organ in the mouth. It is used for taste, swallowing, speech. This organ ...'

'Stop, you bloody article!' But it wouldn't, no matter how many times I flicked the switch. At length I lost my patience with it and belted it, knocking it to the floor. It shattered, spilling out all sorts of little square flakes with dots on them. I put my hands over my mouth and backed out of the room. Whatever shall I tell Jena? I stood looking at the pieces, then at the blue light that curtained Jena's office door.

'There has been a slight accident, Jena.'

The blue light extinguished and Jena said, 'I did not hear you properly, Jan.'

I popped my head round the door frame, repeating my statement. Her eyes scanned me quickly as she asked, 'What kind of accident?'

'The robot isn't well.'

She rubbed her forehead with her finger tips and asked, 'What has happened now?'

'Well, the switch wouldn't work and it wouldn't shut up, so I hit it. Only a tap, and its innards spewed out all over the floor. It wasn't any good. You said it was old, but it just wouldn't shut up. Honest, Jena.'

'Be silent, Jan, and show me.'

I followed her to my room where we both stood looking at it.

'It's dead, Jena. Well and truly dead.'

She shook her head and told me to bring her some tea while she cleared it away.

We sat at the table sipping our tea. She seemed lost in thought. Then suddenly she said, 'Promise me, Jan, if you enter my office, never touch my consoles. I will be very angry if you break them.'

'It was an accident, Jena.'

She sat back and laughed at me. 'You murdered it, Jan.'

I couldn't help but laugh with her, but I also couldn't help thinking that was my first and last robot.

The days turned to weeks and time passed pleasantly in Jena's company. I had no need for a robot to talk to. We spent many hours talking and reading my log-book. She answered all my questions, provided they were kept to a tutor-pupil relationship. Try as I might, she would not let me speak of Karl, although she did let me rattle on about my days as a trooper. All part of my memory enhancement, I suppose.

'I think that is sufficient tutoring for today, Jan,' she said as she walked towards her office.

Well, I'll be blowed! I had enjoyed those past few weeks so

much that I hadn't realised that crafty devil was schooling me! Pity all schooling couldn't be so pleasurable.

'When do I have to meet the Dwellers?' I called.

She returned to the door. 'You are not ready yet. I will tell you when. I most certainly am not looking forward to the encounter.'

I wasn't going to push it. The thought of meeting the Dweller that killed old Karshaa angered me. I think the handlers should have shot it and saved Karshaa, but as Jena had told me, another young bull would have challenged him.

'Would you like guests this evening, Jan?'

'Who, Jena, who is coming?'

'Karl and Virg.'

'Oh, my favourite and your favourite.'

'How do you feel about meeting them? I promise you they will not venture near you.'

I stared at her, waiting, although I knew not what for.

'I shall be with you, Jan. We really must try to socialise you a little more. If it is too much for Claire in male company, then perhaps we can rethink the situation.'

'I'll try not to let Claire take over because I do love those two Arenians, or ruffians, as you call them.'

She smiled at the term she had used on them in my former life, then she made her exit.

Seven o'clock prompt, Karl and Virg arrived, looking very handsome. Jena greeted them, offering them a place at the table the opposite side to me. Karl's eyes met mine and as he winked he told me he had missed my company. I think I blushed.

'Going to be a trooper, Jan?' asked Virg right out of the blue.

'Stop teasing her, Virg,' Jena told him.

'Nonsense, Jena, Jan was a fine trooper. I would vouch for her skill and loyalty any time.'

I sat staring at him, with waves of memory flashing through my mind.

'I still have the oak log you gave me,' I said hurriedly, and spun on my chair, pointing at its place on a shelf.

'So you have, little Fish, so you have.'

Little Fish: my nickname. I turned and smiled at him. 'I shall always love you, Virg. I was so proud to be part of the family.'

I glanced at Karl who was filling the wine glasses and I said to Jena, 'Can we have the wine you served when I married Karl? It was a lovely smooth drink.'

Karl quickly glanced at me and then to Jena. She grinned and said, 'I think not, Jan, it was not wine but a potion.'

I didn't answer. Looking at her bemused expression was enough to embarrass me.

'Now this is one of the reasons I like eating here,' remarked Virg, looking hungrily at his dinner, 'Young Earthians always get the best choice of food. I think, Jena, that is the reason you do this work.'

'Mushrooms and kidney are Jan's favourite, and I must confess to being rather partial to them also. Now eat, my children, and enjoy.'

I took a mouthful of delicious kidney, and felt a terrible heaving in my tummy. I ran to the toilet and lost it. When I had composed myself, I looked up at Jena who was at hand and almost cried as I told her that Claire didn't like kidney.

Jena looked sad for me but told me how well I was getting along with our company. 'You cannot alter Claire's taste, so do not blame yourself for that. Perhaps I can do something for you later. Now let me get you another meal of your choice.'

I ate fish while my guests enjoyed the kidney and mushrooms. I hated Claire for that moment.

Conversation flowed like wine to be savoured and sustain us. On the odd occasion the men would pat my hand or shoulder as they reminded me of experiences in my former lives. Laughter was abundant when Virg reminded me of how I had been hosed down at the end of my first day as a trooper, and I thought it was an initiation ceremony.

We talked of dream machines and my first robot with its untimely end, which Jena had accused me of murdering. Yes, laughter was plentiful, but the evening had to end. It came like second nature to kiss and be kissed on the cheek by the men I loved like brothers. My first step to accepting Karl.

I was admiring my garden when Jena called me. On returning to her, she introduced me to Jara, a tall, thick-set Arenian.

'Jara is a Master of Dweller handlers. He wishes to speak with you.'

I didn't give him a chance to speak. I said to him aggressively, 'You let them kill my Karshaa, didn't you? You could have put him to sleep peacefully and not let that ape hurt him. You are cruel.'

He stood silently gazing at me, then shook his head in despair. 'My dear child, I had no idea of your fondness for Karshaa, but we cannot intervene when they challenge each other for supremacy. How can I make you understand what a handler feels when he loses a trusted and loyal friend?'

'You loved Karshaa too?' I asked with surprise.

'We were very fond of him, as were all Arenians in his sector. You see, Jan, if we had painlessly destroyed him, that would have left the herd without a leader, and the fight for supremacy could have involved two or more males, with devastating consequences. If it is any consolation to you, my dear, his favourite female stayed by his side to the end.'

I began to weep for Karshaa and his mate. Jena tried to console me while Jara paced the room, obviously embarrassed by my tears.

'This is a natural reaction by Earthlings,' Jena explained to Jara. 'She will get over it soon.'

'I had no intentions of distressing her so.'

'Emotions run high with Earthlings. You will get used to it if you are around them for any length of time,' stated Jena.

'I shall return again to talk to Jan. She is obviously not ready to meet the Dwellers. They would sense her animosity. Would you like me to bring you a photograph of Karshaa the next time I visit you, Jan?'

Jena accepted his offer for me and showed Jara out. As my tears still flowed, Jena stood staring at me then said, 'To think he came to warn you not to upset his apes when next you meet them. Now he has left more concerned for you than his apes. I do not think he will look forward to his next meeting with you, he has never seen an Earthling cry before.'

'I did love Karshaa, you know, even if he did stink.'

Jena laughed at me, saying, 'It is not wise to go to the surface until you are familiarized with the Dwellers, but I will take you to visit a friend tomorrow.'

'Who? Fern?'

'We will see when tomorrow comes.'

'You have ten minutes to drink your tea and be ready before an escort comes for us,' said Jena.

'Why an escort, aren't you coming with me?'

'No one may travel without an escort today, there are repair works on the rails and there may be diversions.'

I was barely ready when the door buzzed. Jena asked the guard to identify himself, but a woman's voice came via the speaker.

'I am the Amazon Saylong One Nine, your escort.'

Jena gagged my mouth and whispered urgently, 'Whatever happens, do not speak unless spoken to. Promise me, Jan?'

I nodded, then she let me go and opened the door.

Dear Mother of Arena, I almost leaped into Jena's arms when I saw the Amazon. Never have I seen such a tall woman: she must have been as tall as any male Arenian and armed like a walking arsenal. She had a hand laser gun on each hip, knives on the sides of her boots, metal wrist bands, metal elbow joints, and a thick leather breast armour with a silver circular necklace on it that also covered her shoulders. Her uniform was brown and her hair was iron grey, plaited to circle her head with a brown band to keep it in place. She looked ready to do battle with anyone. Needless to say, I kept very silent.

Jena did not greet her with an arm shake, she just stated our destination and we followed the giant.

There was little conversation between the two women, but when the Amazon spoke of me to Jena, she referred to me as *it*. It was obvious that there was no love lost between us.

A guard stood at a tunnel junction and directed us to take a left turn. 'The rail cars are working in that section. Other tunnels are dangerous with low intelligence robots working in them.'

Saylong nodded to him and Jena thanked him. On reaching a car, a guard asked Saylong if she wished him to relieve her of her duties, saying he was quite free to resume them for her. She nodded to him and Jena thanked her for her time.

'I am a hunter, not a guard to that!' she said, pointing at me. Then she left us.

I breathed a great sigh of relief on seeing her depart and, smiling at the guard, I whispered a thank you.

The guard asked Jena her destination and told the car to proceed to it.

'I knew Saylong was not pleased with the guard duties. The Amazons are having a blood contest on Saturday, so there is much to occupy them at this time.'

'Will you be attending the spectacle?' asked Jena.

'There will not be room. I shall watch it on the viewing screen.'

'What is a blood contest?' I asked.

The car stopped and my question went unanswered. Jena thanked the guard and told me all my questions would be answered later.

I was sadly disappointed to see it was only Minu we were visiting, but he made us most welcome.

'I do hope your journey was not too tedious, Jena?'

'The obstructions were the least of my worries, Minu. We were escorted here by an Amazon.'

'She was a giant,' I interrupted, 'and they are going to bleed each other on Saturday.'

Minu smiled and said, 'If you behave, then perhaps Jena will let you watch the bouts on the viewing screen.'

I was quite excited about all this and threw my questions at them.

As we sipped tea, Minu told me of the Amazons that roam the tunnels to keep Arena safe. The awful thing was, their main quarry was Earth people who had escaped, but the worst thing was, the Amazons took no live prisoners. They hunted and played cat and mouse with their victims, answering only to their leader, President Tamlarr, for their actions.

Jena began to tell Minu of my meeting with Karl and Virg, but I interrupted her to ask more about the Amazons.

'Later Jan,' said Minu. 'You were saying, Jena?'

'I was saying how well Jan is socializing with the men, but it is very much a brother and sister relationship. Oh yes, Minu, Claire's taste buds leave a lot to be desired. Claire does not like kidney, a favourite food of Jan's, and I must admit to being quite fond of it myself,' she said with a teasing grin.

'I must see what I can do for you, Jena.' As Minu spoke he walked to the far side of the room and opened a drawer. 'Do you remember those pretty stones I showed you, Jan?'

I attempted to rise from the armchair to follow him, but Jena's hand rested on my shoulder to stop me, so I called across to him that I did. I glanced about the room and noticed the clock: eleven thirty. The morning had almost gone, I thought.

'There,' said Minu, opening his hand. 'Now what do you think of them? See the colours within this one? Look, there is a diamond in this one, see, it sparkles like a star.'

'Like ... a ... star,' I heard myself repeat.

'Did you like them?' he asked.

'Yes,' I whispered, reluctant to take my gaze from them.

'My word,' came Jena's voice, 'it is one o'clock already. Jan must be getting hungry, I know I am.'

Minu requested a guard for us and we journeyed home. Jena was right. I was hungry and we sat at the table to enjoy a plate of kidney and mushrooms.

'I am so pleased Claire likes kidney, Jan. That is one thing I miss when you are not here.'

How could I argue with that? I don't know how they did it, but I was eating my favourite food again.

After eating we got onto the subject of Amazons again. Jena told me they never carry any of their children, they are all cloned and Earthlings do their carrying for them. They revere these Earthians and take great care of them. Nothing within reason is too good for them. They also have great respect for their own bodies and it is because of the building of muscles that they cannot and will not carry a child. But for all their worshipping of physique, they use the barbaric ritual of drawing blood from each other in combat. No challenge goes unanswered with them and they obey no one but their President. Fortunately, she sits on the high council and is ruled by the Mother of Arena. Jena also told me that if ever I am near an Amazon, I must always step aside for her to pass. No one may block their path, a rule they have imposed on all who stand in their way. I hope I never meet another Amazon!

That evening, I retired to my room to write in my log-book for the day. Jena asked me if I would like a table-top computer to enter my log into. I was thrilled at the idea, but told her I could not type. She assured me that Claire was quite competent at typing. I awaited my new toy.

Two days later it was put in my room and I gloated over it. 'I have an office like you now, Jena,' I said.

She smiled and proceeded to show me how it worked. She was quite good on the keyboard and with Claire's knowledge of it, I reckoned I would make a pretty good show of things.

'Oh no!' I cried. I shouted, stomped my feet and beat my fists on the desk. Nothing would make me a typist. Jena tried to calm me in order to tell her what the problem was. Eventually she shook me hard, threatening me with punishment, so I sat and wept. I looked wounded at Jena and said, 'It's all Claire's fault. She is left-handed and while I am concentrating on my right hand, she is thinking left hand. Nothing works.'

Jena led me into the sitting room and brought me tea.

'I shall have them take the machine away. I will not have you upsetting yourself over a trivial thing like this, when there is an obvious solution to the problem.'

26

'I'll never be able to type like you, Jena. It's the most mixed up feeling I have ever had.'

'Stop crying and I will let you come into my office with me.'

I felt she had stooped to bribery for a quiet life. I loved her too much to become a burden to her, so I dried my eyes and apologized for my bad temper. She took me into her workroom with all its computers around the walls.

'Do you remember this one?' she asked.

'Oh yes. That's the computer I put my finger on the screen of and guided it through the wall into my bedroom. But why do you have so many computers?'

That was when I got a true picture of what a computer could do. The reason she had so many was because she used so many chips at one time. One computer was merely to talk to other Arenians, like a view phone. Then came the highlight. She pressed a key on the console and said, 'I would like a computer for Jan to speak to.'

As she spoke, so the words came up on the screen. Then she pushed another key and the machine read her words back to her. I swooned and let out a gasp of, 'Oh, yes please!'

'Give me a day or two and I will see what I can do for you,' was all she said, but it was like magic. She made me promise that evening that when I used my new computer, I would switch it to manual every few paragraphs and type a sentence to keep a skill that Claire had worked hard to master.

'I would like you to become an accomplished typist,' she told me.

I thoroughly enjoyed filling in my log-book and having it read back to me via earphones. When Karl came, I really showed off with my new toy. Karl smiled at me sweetly and said, 'Our children already use such machines quite skilfully.'

I hadn't given any thought to my children of my previous lives and it made me think back to them. 'Do you visit them, Karl?'

'Of course I do, my dear.'

'Do they ever mention me?'

'Only April. She has a different temperament to her brother's and sister's, which creates a problem at times for her tutor.'

I held my head low with shame for not giving them my time, or for that matter, my thoughts. I looked up at him and whispered, 'I love them just as I love you and all that is Arenian. It's just that, it isn't a love I want to touch. Do you understand what I mean?'

He stroked my hair back and cupped my face in his hands, saying, 'I love you, my little Jan. I will always be here for you. Come to me when you feel you have the need for companionship. I will never turn away from you.'

My eyes watered and I sank my head on to his chest. His arms encircled me and his strength made me feel secure. Slowly he released me, leading me into the sitting room and bringing three cups of tea. Jena automatically walked from her place of work to join us, as though anticipating our moves. Of course, I had forgotten at that moment about her computer that could spy on my every move.

'Thank you for the tea, Karl. What do you think of Jan's new skill at typing? Personally, I am quite pleased with her. I no longer have to tell her to give more time to her log-book. However, I am going to insist on a reader of logs to ensure Jan catches up on her past lives.'

I wasn't happy about that. After all, it was a lot of remembering and I was having to contend with Claire's thoughts also. But complaining to Jena about such things only strengthened her argument on the subject. So the next few days were very tearful as the reader of logs, a female Arenian named Tyne, read my life and innermost thoughts to me. At the end of each day, I felt sapped of energy and was glad of my bed, where I would cry myself to sleep. Jena always sat by my bed until sleep came. I don't know what I would have done without her.

It had been all worthwhile. I was stronger and more positive for the time the reader had spent with me. My talks with Jena enhanced my awareness of Arena and I felt more able to face life. I only wish it could have moulded my temperament also, for I was still fiery of nature and full of all the discrepancies of human nature. For instance, I was permitted to enter Jena's office to watch her using her computers, on the understanding I kept quiet and told no one.

'In that bottom drawer Jan, I keep a cleaning kit for my screens. Will you get it for me please?'

I opened the drawer and much to my surprise I saw a teddy bear lying there. 'What is this doing here?' I asked.

'Oh, that belonged to my last ward. I had intended throwing it away. Put it in the disposer, Jan.'

'Ward, what ward? Who was she and what was she doing here? You're my mum. I live here!'

Jena swung round in her chair to face me. 'Put it in the disposer and we will say no more about it.'

'Who was she and did she call you Mum like I do? How long was she here and did ...'

'Enough!'

'This is my home.'

'I said that is enough!'

I stared at the bear and whispered, 'I bet she never loved you.'

Jena rose from her chair to approach me and I stepped back in fear of her anger. I glanced up quickly and noticed she was no longer in a rage. Her look was firm but understanding. I felt the tears well up and I turned away from her as my shoulders jerked with my sobs.

'All this silly talk of a child that is no longer with us. You are a strange breed. I am always here for your awakening, I never fail you. It is my duty to work with Earthians. I cannot be idle for a year or more, waiting for you to complete your transition. My work must go on. Now put these silly Earth feelings away and I will forget all about your childish outburst.'

I turned and cuddled her until my tears subsided, then I sat and admired the bear, asking if I might keep it.

CHAPTER FOUR
GETTING TO KNOW HIM

Although I never mentioned any wards that Jena might have cared for, the bear, fond as I was of it, was a constant reminder that others had shared her affections. I was jealous.

Jara arrived one morning with a photo of Karshaa, as promised. I was over the moon with it. Then he handed me another ape's photo; on one side of its face it had a bad scar.

'Who is this?' I asked.

'Vindaar, Karshaa's rival. An Earth man did that to him with a laser gun.'

'You killed the Earth swine, didn't you?'

'No, the apes killed him.'

'Good boy, Vindaar. How dare they torture you!' I said, almost stroking the photo of Karshaa's slayer.

'You can keep the photographs, Jan, and Jena will bring you to visit Vindaar when she has time to do so.' He bid us goodbye and left.

'Well, young lady, how do you feel about meeting the Dwellers?'

'I don't mind, Jena. But I do mind about people hurting them. They are quite inoffensive apes really.'

'Just a little like you, Jan, short on patience.'

'No I'm not,' I said with a whine. She just laughed at me.

'Make the best of your morning, Jan. Falo is coming this afternoon.'

'Oh hell, must she?'

'Just do as she bids and all will go well.'

I sidled up to Jena and asked, 'Why does she always find fault with me, or do all messengers find fault with everyone?'

'Messengers seek perfection, Jan, and perfection is hard to find.'

'I just wish she wasn't coming.'

Falo did arrive that afternoon and I stayed close to Jena. I felt a bit of a fraud judging her the way I had; she was so pleased with me, taking interest in all I was doing and showing pleasure in my typewriting skills. She picked up the teddy bear from my pillow and said to Jena, 'If the child has the nursing instinct, then I see no reason why she should not be coupled. She is strong enough to breed.'

'I am responsible for Jan and I will not have her put at risk.'

'Then, Jena, I think you should relinquish your guardianship of the child and let another guardian take her, who will have the girl coupled.'

I stood wide-eyed, watching the two women do battle over me. The thought of losing Jena made me very afraid, to the point of shouting, 'No Falo, no! I would rather die than be parted from Jena.'

'There is your biggest mistake ,Jena,' said Falo, 'to let an Earthling become too attached.'

'On the contrary, Falo, that is the factor that separates Earthians from Arenians: their uncontrollable desires. I will not allow you to hurt her in this way.'

'I dislike being challenged, Jena, but I must confess, you are one of the few to do so. I find it most stimulating.'

Jena smiled at Falo, who returned the compliment.

'Perhaps next time, Falo, we can have our discussion out of the child's hearing. This has distressed her.' Falo nodded and took her leave of us.

I threw my arms around Jena and told her how clever she was.

'Never underestimate Falo, Jan. She will take the matter further.'

'You mean they could take me away?'

'No, dear, but it is possible your breeding date might be brought forward.'

I felt afraid as I thought of Falo, who could be Jekyll or Hyde, so I retreated into my garden and sought out the big oak tree to bare my soul to. What would I do without my garden as a sanctuary?

Two days later, while we were having breakfast, Jena broke the news to me that the council's orders were that I must start breeding with Karl. I sat staring at Jena. It was like being told I had a terminal illness. She rested her hand on mine and told me, 'In six months a lot can happen.' She said she was more concerned for Claire, because she knew Jan trusted her judgement. I half smiled and agreed with her. I knew she would not let me face this alone. It had ruined my appetite for breakfast though, so I left the table.

'Well, my dear, you at least have something new to enter into your log-book.'

'I could have thought of better things. Claire is so afraid of men. Oh she would love to have a baby, but she is childish enough to want to conceive without the mating ritual.'

'If in the time allotted, Jan, we cannot change Claire, and I promise I will do all I can, will you accept artificial insemination, my dear?'

'Yes, Jena, but please do everything in your power to cure her of this fear. There are times when I want my Karl so much.'

'We will work something out. Now forget all this upset and come with me.' She took me by the hand and led me into her work room, promising to show me some of the magic of Arena. I loved being permitted to see her working and living quarters, especially when she played her guitar to me.

'You think your talking computer is wonderful, Jan? Let me show you the machine that dreams are made of.' She sat me opposite a viewing screen, switched it to record and as she placed a headband around her head, she told me she must have silence. She sat down and closed her eyes. I wasn't sure what would happen or whether to look at Jena or the screen. A long moment passed and the screen came alive. It was me sitting at the table asking Jena to do all she could to help me and cure Claire. Then the picture changed and Jara was asking me how I felt about meeting his Dwellers.

The screen went blank and Jena took off the headband. I sat looking blankly at her.

'Well Jan,' she said as she pressed a couple of buttons on

the viewer and the film repeated itself, 'what do you think of that?'

I never said a word. I watched the screen, then I looked at her and still I was unable to speak. Jena beamed a broad grin at me and explained that that was how Arenians record their memories for their log-books, all on chips. You can imagine the excitement I felt when I was able to speak again, but she would not let me try it because it could be dangerous without the training and time it took to get used to it. I had seen a miracle. I could think of nothing else.

'One of life's secrets,' she said. 'No matter how hurtful life may be, Jan, there is always a new day not far away.'

'Or my mum in the next room,' I added with pride.

She brought two teas and we sat, elbows on table, sipping away, my mind on Falo's visit and the problems I was having with Claire. 'I don't really know what to do, Jena. It is all too much for me to work out.'

'What is, Jan? Tell me and I will try to help you.'

'It's Claire, Jena. When I am alone, all I want to do is be with my Karl. I didn't think it was possible for a person to hold so much love. I want Karl so much that it hurts and I can't wait to pour that love on him when he visits. Why must wanting hurt so? When he enters the room it's as though Claire encircles me and all that love melts away and becomes brotherly love.' I began to weep. Amidst my tears I told her that I had even thought of asking her for some of the wine to intoxicate me as it had on my wedding day to Karl.

'The potion cannot work alone, Jan. The mind must be also tuned and enhanced. Go to your room, dear, and rest.'

'What good will that do? I would rather go to my garden.'

'You have been honest with me, Jan. If it is my help you are seeking, then you must trust me also. Now go to your room and relax. I will be in there very soon to help you. Dry your eyes and do as I ask.'

I went to my bedroom and lay down, wondering what Jena could say or do to drive Claire away. I couldn't live with Claire, or without her. What a terrible dilemma to be in!

Jena came to me as promised, sitting herself on the side of my bed. We chatted about Claire's likes and dislikes, and how they hindered me. Jena spoke of me and Karl as though she was talking to Claire. Her voice drifted as though a door had closed between us. A peacefulness crept over me, a contentment. If this was a dream, then I wanted it to last forever. I had the feeling that I had known this sensation before, perhaps in the dark corridors of time between my lives. I savoured the warm cradle-like feeling as sleep caressed my senses and endless time slipped by and comforted me.

'Jan, your favourite dinner is being served. Wake up, sleepy-head! Are you hungry?'

'For kidney and mushrooms, you bet!'

'You slept for four hours. Isn't it surprising what crying can do for you Earthlings? Still, there are better things to come. Tomorrow we will visit the Dwellers, and in the evening Karl is visiting you.'

'Oh boy, roll on tomorrow!'

I looked hard at the photo of Vindaar. I felt no hatred of him for killing Karshaa. Like dogs, there has to be a hierarchy, but I felt ashamed that an Earthian had caused Vindaar so much pain. I only hoped he wouldn't think to avenge himself on me, another Earthian.

Next day I travelled with Jena to the level of the great apes accompanied by three of their handlers. 'Where is Jara?' I asked a handler.

'He is supervising in another sector. I will be supervising here. You will do as you are told, is that understood?'

Jena assured him that I would be punished if I disobeyed. I glanced at her and kept silent. The gates of the lift slid open and the lead handler sounded the gong. At that point I stood closer to Jena, gripping her hand. Her arm came round my shoulders as she gently patted me. Gently she spoke, telling me how privileged I was to be protected by such wonderful creatures. As though time was their servant, they sauntered our way, unhurried and almost oblivious of our presence, their nostrils doing most of their investigating for them.

34

'Vindaar,' called the handler. 'Come, Vindaar.' The lead bull came alive and quickened his pace. I froze. Jena's patting hand changed to a massaging movement on my shoulder.

'Isn't he beautiful, Jan?' she said quietly. I wanted to run, but Jena's grip was firm and a handler joined us to reinforce Jena's grip.

'Vindaar,' said the handler, 'come and show me your poorly face.' The great monster sat on his haunches for the handler to inspect him. That did it for me. My heart melted, as did my fear. Slowly I walked forward and with a handler's guidance, my hand was placed by Vindaar's nose. I waited for the long process of inspection by smell, then I ruffled his head and rested my head on his chest whispering, 'I'm so sorry for what those bad people did to you, my boy.' A heavy arm rested on my shoulder, drawing me to him. He almost deafened me as he sniffed my neck and ears.

'I won't hurt you Vindaar,' I said with a grunt in my voice from his great weight. He rose to his full height and I thought I was going to die as he swung his arms and beat his chest. A handler steadied me as my balance faulted, then the handler rested my hand on Vindaar's chest.

'He has accepted you, Jan. Now no one will hurt you in his domain.'

The handler let me go and following them, we mingled with the great beasts. A handler told me not to show too much affection to Vindaar's subordinates, that privilege was his alone. Humans must save their affections for him alone.

As cautiously as we had entered, so we left and my first thought on returning home was to shower and wash my hair. For the next couple of hours, I kept pestering Jena to check my hair for fleas or crawlies; it kept itching. It was all in my mind, she told me as she scratched at her shoulder and laughed at me.

Karl arrived for dinner. I stood in the centre of the room feasting my eyes on him. He looked different, even more handsome, in fact perfect.

'Hello my little lady,' he said as he came to me and kissed my forehead. 'So the apes love you. But not as much as I do, my pet.'

We sat to eat, but I was full of the day's events while my companions nodded and ate. 'Have you had something done to your hair, Karl? You look different,' I said.

Karl smiled at Jena mischievously and said, 'Well done and thank you.'

'I think so too,' she said and rose to clear the table. I didn't know what they were talking about, I just wanted to look at Karl and fathom out why he looked so much nicer.

Dinner dispensed with, Karl moved to the settee and pulled me down beside him. Wine was served and we had a pleasant evening chatting, with the odd rough and tumble with Karl and me. It was time for him to leave, but I begged him to stay longer. He did, only fifteen minutes and then Jena thought it prudent to part us. He promised to visit again soon.

Life was great. I pestered Jena to let me see her moving picture log-book work and was embarrassed to have the picture of Karl and me getting a little familiar with each other on the settee. I hung my head, aware of my blushes as I apologised to her. She only laughed.

I had thought Karl looked different, but I was aware that I felt different and I liked the feeling.

CHAPTER FIVE
THE HILL FARMERS

One day Jena said to me: 'Karl has contacted me, Jan. He wishes to know if you would like to accompany him on an excursion?' I wasn't going to miss out on being in his company, so it was a definite yes.

'Where are we going?' I kept asking him. Hell, would he tell me? No, not a thing except to say 'shopping'.

Now how can you go shopping on a world where money is obsolete? Bloody silly, if you ask me. Never mind, his company was enough for me.

We travelled quite some time on two rail cars at a heck of a speed and it wasn't until we came to a station where we had to change our clothing that I realised we were going to the surface. It took a little longer than expected, because of the difficulty in finding clothes my size. I looked at Karl and said, 'Dodgy going to the surface with all those Stonies. Bad news, man.'

'Why should that worry you, Jan? You were an excellent trooper.'

'Well I suppose with a hand laser each and a goodly size leg knife, we could give a pretty good account of ourselves.'

He beamed a beautiful smile at me, slapped me on the back and said, 'We are so good, we do not even need any weapons.'

We were like a couple of kids as we made our way to the surface and boarded a luxury coach which travelled in a convoy. It was then that he told me that we were going to a village outpost where Arenians traded with the Hill Farmers. I'd never heard of them, but apparently they were friendly while the Arenians supplied them with the equipment they couldn't obtain for themselves. I imagined them to be big hairy cavemen clad in animal skins and carrying clubs for weapons.

The convoy drew to a halt by lots of little mounds, scattered over the ground.

'What are they, Karl, ant hills?'

'No, they are the little hills the farmers live in.'

The guard alighted from the transport and only then did the Farmers emerge from their little hills.

'Midgets,' I said with surprise. 'Bloody little midgets.'

They had spears, choppers, bows and arrows. I've never seen the like before. It was like something out of a comic book. What a let-down; I didn't know whether to laugh or cry.

'Surely they aren't the Farmers you talked about, are they?'

'Yes, Jan, and they can be bad-tempered creatures, so do not do anything to upset them. Those weapons they carry are tipped with poison, they will use them if provoked.'

'Where are their farms and animals?'

'Very few of them eat meat. They gather all wild plants, they are quite expert in herbal medicines.'

'I'm not surprised they are so small if they don't get meat rations.'

One brave little man walked among us saying, 'What you brought to trade, Boss?' His questions were for anyone whose ears they fell upon. He poked an Arenian's leg and said, 'What you got, Boss?' The Arenian told him he wanted to inspect the Farmer's trade first, and the little man led him away.

We wandered about looking in little doorways and getting pleasant smiles from the Farmers' womenfolk. One little lady sat outside her door nursing a baby and as I bent over to look at the child, she clutched the child tightly and said angrily, 'No trade, no trade.' Karl pulled me away, waving his hand to signal we didn't want the child. In spite of her unwarranted anger at me, I felt a terrible pity for her and wished I could have done something to reassure her of my good intentions.

Someone pulled my finger and a Farmer asked, 'What you got, Boss?'

I shrugged and said, 'What you got, Boss?'

He gave me a crafty wink and indicated for me to follow him.

38

'Can I go over there, Karl?'

'Alright, pet, I'll be just there if you need me,' he said, pointing at another hill.

I followed the little man as he led me into his hill. His lady came to the door and made me welcome. Bending low, I entered a well laid out little room. Considering the floor was earth, the place was quite tidy with different coloured pieces of material to cover seats and walls. Farmer pointed to a seat for me, then pushed his wife, who came back to us with tin cups of drink. I wasn't happy about drinking it. Farmer smiled and raised his cup, then drank. So I did the same, but I only sipped mine. Sugar water, I thought. No, it leaves the mouth too dry.

'Mmmm,' I said. 'Mmmm.'

A little face appeared from behind a hanging cloth and I wiggled my fingers at the child. He ran out all coy to his mother's lap. The Farmer pulled cloth and wood from part of the floor, uncovering a hole with his possessions in it, all the time giving me crafty grins. He took out little bundles of cloth, gently unfolding them and spreading them out. Stuck to the centre of each piece of cloth, making the most beautiful pictures, were twigs, petals, leaves and grass. Whatever the land and its seasons had to offer, the Farmer had used to create beauty once again.

'What you want, Boss?' he asked me. He could see how wondrous I thought they were. What could I say, or what did I have for him?

'Who made them?' I asked, not taking my gaze from them.

'Me, Boss, me.' As I looked up he was pointing to his wife and himself.

'Clever,' I smiled at them. 'Now I find other Boss to come and look. You wait, yes? Wait!'

I went to look for Karl. Damn, where was he? I went to a guard and told him my problems. 'Take me to the hill and I will negotiate a deal for you,' he said.

I took him, but I hadn't a clue what I would pay with.

As the guard entered, he greeted the dwarves like old friends. 'Hello, Kimja, hello, Arrill. How is baby Lootock?'

'All good, Boss.' said the little man, quite flustered with excitement. He pushed his wife to make room for the guard.

'Is this what you have chosen, Earthling?'

'Yes, I'm hoping my guardian will like them.'

'I am sure she will. You must be very fond of her. What is your name?'

'Jan the Arenian, and yours?'

'Akso. This family is well known to me. Kimja is not easy to bargain with, but I know what he likes. Salt, Kimja?'

Kimja grinned craftily and said, 'Hide, Boss, fish?'

Akso raised his hand to stop the little man asking for more and said, 'I'll bring them for you, Kimja.'

Kimja wasn't about to miss out on anything. He followed the guard and me to a truck, and as Akso gave him a bag of salt, a bag of dried fish and a roll of thick leather, so the little man pointed out other goodies he wanted. If the truck hadn't been so high, I think Kimja would have taken the lot. He staggered away, his arms full. I turned to Akso and asked, 'Do you have anything for his wife and child? Just a little something?'

Akso smiled at me and reached for two more bundles. 'Needles and thread for Arrill and chew sweets for Lootock.'

'Thank you, Akso, most kind of you.'

I ran to the hill and got there in time to see Arrill helping Kimja with his treasure. I do believe Kimja thought I had changed my mind, because he pushed all the stuff into a corner and stood in front of it, as though to protect it. I held out the two bundles, offering them to Arrill, indicating that one was for their child. Arrill unwrapped them with great care and rushed about the room with delight.

With slow deliberate movements, Kimja folded my presents and gave them to me. We thanked each other many times and I left the hill to search for Karl. As I searched, someone pulled at my clothing; it was Arrill. She offered me a small bundle. I opened it to see dried herbs.

'Thank you, Arrill, but what are they for?'

'Make you brown like others,' she replied, pointing at my face.

I bent down and gripped her hand. 'Thank you, Arrill. I will come and see you again one day.' Then she shyly hurried away.

Eventually I found Karl tossing large stones into a circle. 'What are you doing, Karl?'

'Trying to beat these little perishers.'

'Who's winning?'

'They are!'

I managed to drag him away, leaving three disgruntled dwarves dividing the booty they had won from Karl and two guards. The dwarves were almost fighting each other as they decided who would have what. Strange little folk!

'The sun is on its downward journey,' said Akso to Karl. 'Time we journeyed also.'

We were told to board the coach. We left the Hill Farmers to fight and argue over their new possession. We were asked to leave all gifts with our surface clothing and our name and number with them. We were told we would receive them the next day. I was disappointed. I had so looked forward to giving Jena her pictures made from wild plants.

A shower, dinner, pleasant conversation and bed made my day complete. Karl had promised to pick up the presents and bring them for me the next day.

I was very excited when he entered the apartment, but his look was one of disappointment. He explained that the presents I bought were not checked, just cleansed. Unfortunately, when they were unwrapped, they were a mess of goo and slime. I looked at Jena; I could have cried with disappointment.

'The next time they send a trading convoy to the Hill Farmers, Jan, I promise Karl will take you. If you must bring me a present, then I suggest you bring a wood carving. I understand they are quite expert at sculpture.'

So much for my good intentions!

I told Jena about the herbs Arrill had given me, to make me brown like Arenians. 'Why are Arenians so brown and healthy-looking, Jena?'

'Because of our genes. We evolved from dark-skinned people. It is our natural pigment. If I did not live below ground, I would be much darker skinned. There are many Arenians that are very dark-skinned.'

'So you are not a white woman?'

'I do not think any Arenians are.'

That left me gob-smacked. But she was still my mum.

Karl stayed to dinner that day. There was no fear from Claire. It was wonderful being able to be close to him. It made my wanting him more apparent to Jena. She told me if I could restrain my feelings a little longer, then my patience would be rewarded.

The door alarm sounded and the person outside addressed herself as Zarr One Eight. Jena smiled as she activated her belt lock, opening the door to the Arenian I had known as Aunt Mildred. They welcomed each other warmly and Zarr handed Jena a large box. Jena opened it to reveal a pendulum clock. Together the women assembled it and as Jena held it up to show me, she said, 'Well, Jan, do you like it?'

I couldn't help but smile at her pleasure. 'It's an old Earth clock. What is so special about it?'

Zarr came to me and after asking if I was well and was I happy, she told me she had just returned from Earth where such clocks were plentiful. On Arena, they are prized by collectors.

'Where are you going to hang it, Jena?' I asked.

'In my quarters,' she replied.

'Thank goodness. I don't think I could live with that constant loud ticking.'

'It chimes also,' laughed Zarr.

'You'll be sorry, Jena!'

They retired into Jena's rooms for what seemed an age. As Zarr left I asked if she had seen my Earth husband, Jim.

'No, Jan. That was not my assignment.' Then she left.

A man came the next day to fit Jena's clock on the wall of her sitting room. I only heard it chime from my living room if I listened hard. Funny people, I thought. Will I ever understand Arenians?

'Jan, I have to leave the apartment for a few hours tomorrow. Would you like Asta to stay with you?'

'I have a choice?'

'I cannot leave you alone. Of course, Karl can stay with you, if you so wish.'

'Ah yes, now you are talking my kind of language. Karl will do fine.'

'You do realise, Jan, that you are not permitted to mate?'

'I know I know, but it will be soon, won't it?'

'Very soon, Jan. I am pleased to see the way you have handled Claire.'

The morrow came and with it my handsome Karl. Jena readied herself and gave Karl his last instructions, ie see that Jan has sufficient to eat and keep any activities to a minimum.

'Oh go, Jena! I shall probably wind up taking care of Karl.'

She gave me one last glance which said 'behave', and she was gone. Only then did a strange feeling of concern fill me. She never leaves me unless something is wrong, I thought. She had left me when I was a trooper and something wasn't right then.

'Where has Jena gone, Karl?'

'Where Jena goes and what she does is Jena's business.'

'Something isn't right, Karl.'

'Come here and let me hold you. Did you know that we can be husband and wife soon?'

'Yes, I know all that, but I just wish Jena would confide in me a little more. I do worry about her, you know.'

He drew me close to him and very seriously said, 'You are growing up, Jan. Jena has gone for a medical examination. We all have them, but I do not think she will take kindly to me telling her subordinate. Can I rely on your discretion, Jan?'

I slipped my arms around him as I looked up at him. 'Karl, all I want to know is that the people I love are safe and well. Now I'm happy.'

For the next five hours, I enjoyed his company. The moments were passionate with desires as we investigated each other's bodies, but never a fulfilment. He would not permit a joining of us. At least I would be able to meet Jena's eyes when she asked me if I had behaved myself.

When she returned, I found myself trying to anticipate her every move in order to lighten her workload. At length she said, 'Karl told you where I have been!'

'She was concerned about you, Jena, and would not settle until she knew you were well. Jan sensed the situation.'

'Perhaps Falo was correct. We are becoming too close.'

'To hell with Falo!' I cried. 'A family should confide in each other if we are to help each other in times of need. Are you ill, Jena?'

'Not as such, Jan. I need a bone replacement.' She smiled at me and added, 'Some parts wear out with age.'

'Don't worry, Jena. You tell me what you want doing and I'm your girl. Karl can do the heavy jobs.'

He grinned at Jena and said, 'Now that is an offer you should not refuse. She has it all worked out. Do not dismiss such good intentions.'

Karl stayed for dinner, leaving Jena and I alone at eight-thirty.

'Jena, when they put a new bone in you, will it be from an Earthian?'

'Certainly not. We clone and grow our own limbs.'

'Oh Mother, you mean somewhere there is a room with parts of people growing, like arms and legs?'

'It is very easy to grow limb parts and graft them. But why do you worry about such things when you yourself are reborn via memories from your brain to your donor?'

'My what?'

'Claire's body is a host's body. You will use it until you require a replacement. Just as you used Mellanie's body.'

'I know I'm reborn, but who thinks about such things as hosts and donors? I don't!'

'Minu does. He is the doctor that finds you a suitable host at short notice. Without Arenians like Minu, you could not be reborn.'

I sat silent, trying to make sense of what she had told me.

'Was your last ward, the one who had the teddy bear, reborn?'

'No.'

'Only me?'

'Yes.'

I sat back, feeling quite smug for being the chosen one. She must love me more than all the others, I thought. I had been right to choose her for my mum.

'I have told you things this evening that a guardian never discusses with her ward. Now I will have no more questions, Jan. Go to bed.'

I thought that was the end of my evening, but not a bit of it. I lay in bed for hours thinking over all I had learned. But sleep and sweet dreams came as I thought of my Karl and the wonderful day we had shared together. Soon we would be as one.

Almost a week had passed when Karl and Virg arrived one afternoon quite unannounced.

'This is an unexpected pleasure,' said Jena as she let them in. 'I take it there is a very good reason for this visit. Could it possibly be the kidney and mushrooms?'

'That would go down nicely after we have seen the bouts on the viewing screen, Jena,' said Karl.

I dragged them joyfully into the room, making a great fuss of them both. 'What bouts, what's on?'

'We tried to get ringside seats,' said Virg, 'But it was fully booked, so you and a good meal were our next choice, Jena.'

'How nice to know Jan and I were second choice. I am not sure you deserve to be fed.'

I giggled as Virg, like a naughty little boy, tried to persuade Jena to feed them. He even went on his knees.

'Get up, you ruffian,' she said, trying to suppress her pleasure at having his boisterous company. I looked on with delight at seeing them together. Two of my favourite people enjoying each other's company: a golden moment for us all.

'Is anyone going to tell me what is coming on the viewer?' I asked impatiently.

'Amazons, Jan, with a blood bout. Perhaps you are too young to watch it,' said Virg, grinning with devilment.

'Jena?' I said with a whine.

'Pay no attention to him, Jan, he is tormenting you.'

Jena brought us tea while Virg put the viewer on and turned the sound off. 'Another thirty minutes before it starts,' he said.

'Tell me about the family, Virg, are they all well?'

'I do not think you will know any of them, Jan. Those you knew have been recalled to resume their chosen careers.'

'Have they caught Robert yet?'

'Yes, dear. They made him a Thormec and he works for the council now.'

'They trust him to work for Arena. You must be joking?'

'He does as he is told, or dies.'

I did not answer him. I tried to imagine Robert as a subordinate trooper. I couldn't see it working out. He had a mind of his own and a will to match it. It gave me something to think on and I stayed quiet.

Meanwhile, Virg was catching up on all the news from Jena and Karl. It was background chatter that was music to my ears and a warmth to my heart. Then the sound went up on the viewer as we settled back to watch the female giants being introduced. By the Mother, some of them looked positively mean and wild! They didn't fight in a boxing ring as fighters do on Earth. They fought in a large cage, which Karl explained was to protect the onlookers. Their referee, another Amazon, carried a staff with an overgrown boxing glove on either end, which she freely used on the fighters to part them. They were vicious fighters and showed no mercy to a crippled opponent. It was in for the kill and to hell with all else. Even the referee got a thrashing and gave as good back. Most of the bouts were between barefoot, scantily-dressed Amazons. But they all wore leather breast plates and helmets. The frightening bouts were the blooding initiation bouts, where the young warriors wore full weaponry except laser guns. I never realised that the metal elbow, wrist and shoulder joints were not only for protection; when activated, spikes extended from them with devastating consequences. In these bouts, the referee was also fully clad to protect herself.

Jena moved about the room replenishing drinks. I stared transfixed at the screen, while the men punched the air and shouted with excitement. At one point, Virg was on his knees in front of the screen and Karl had to push him aside to see it. How they ate dinner and kept it down after all that excitement, I shall never know. When Virg asked me what I thought of the fights, all I could say was, 'I would rather have an Amazon as a friend than an enemy.'

I told Virg of my visit to the Dwarves and how Karl had told me what bad-tempered people they were. I wondered how they would fare in the company of bad tempered Amazons. 'Do you think the Dwarves would probably become extinct?' I asked.

I was surprised when he told me the Amazons found the Dwarves amusing and teased them in a kindly way, almost like pets. I told him I had made friends with one particular family of Dwarves and the next time I saw them I would give their child my Teddy bear as a present. He said he was on Leave and would take me the following day to see them, with Jena and Karl's approval. So it was settled. Tomorrow I would visit Kimja and family.

The journey was tiring but Virg was good company.

The first thing I did on arriving was to search out Kimja's hill. Only Arrill was at home and she greeted me with a beaming smile, then got all flustered, not knowing how to welcome me.

'Where is Lootock, Arrill?' I asked her.

'Lootock gone, Boss.'

'Is Lootock out with Kimja?'

'No, Boss, Lootock gone. Him snake bite in arm. Him gone, Boss.'

I sank to my knees, letting the wrapped toy fall to the ground. Arrill just stared at my watering eyes. I didn't know whether to cuddle her or just cry. 'Lootock dead?' I whispered.

'Yes, Boss. Him dead. Snake bite here.' She pointed to her arm.

At that moment another Dwarf came and demanded I give something to him also. I ignored him but he took the toy I had intended for Lootock. It served no purpose now. My concern was with Arrill. I took her hand and led her to a truck, asking the guard to give her whatever she needed. The toy-stealing Dwarf returned to me, demanding I give to him also. He snatched a bag of salt from Arrill that enraged me and, letting my boot fly in the direction of his ass, I told him to sod off. This in turn enraged the Dwarf and he ran off with everything Arrill had been given. Now tempers were flying in all directions and my cussing was the loudest. Virg came a-running, as did that thieving sod of a Dwarf. He ran under the truck to collect more booty, but the only boot he got had my foot still in it.

He and I were at war!

'Gotcha, you little bleeder.' Then he was gone again. If I hadn't been so upset at the loss of Arrill's son and the loss of everything we'd tried to give her, then I suppose it might have been funny. But funny wasn't in my vocabulary, only words like, 'I'll kill that little bastard if I catch him'.

Virg and the guard had heard enough and were restraining me. 'Get her on to the couch before she causes a riot,' said the guard. Back came the little git and got in a couple of kicks at me as I struggled to get free.

'Not like She Boss, She Boss no good.'

'I'll give you no good, you short-assed bleeder! I hope your ears get diarrhoea and shit all over you!'

SLAM! The coach door shut and Virg had me pinned in a seat. 'You bad-tempered, foul-mouthed child! If you were still one of my troopers, I would have struck you down. Now you will stay here and keep silent or know my wrath!' All the time he was pointing his finger at me.

I felt sick with anger but kept silent as I held the back of the seat in front of me and made a rocking motion, thinking it would help me rid myself of the frustration.

If I never did see a Dwarf again, it would still be too soon for me!

CHAPTER SIX
ECHO

Jena showed anger on my return, but much to my surprise it was shortlived.

A few days later Karl came to see me and after spending a little time with Jena, he came to me.

'I suppose you heard all about my ungainly behaviour at the Hill Farmers' settlement?' I said.

'Yes, but Jena and I understand how you must have felt. You also lost a child, you were only expressing a mother's feelings.'

I crept into his arms and told him he was as strong as my old oak tree. Together we walked into the garden and stood beneath the oak. I held him and told him of Lootock's fate as I wept. Gently he rocked me until my tears disappeared amidst his gentle lips and caressing hands. Slowly we sank to the grass and among the beauty that surrounded us, he coloured my world with talk of love. Gently he cradled me in his arms and carried me to my bed. As his body rested over mine, I knew there would be no denial of any part of us. There was no beginning of love, just an embracing as we merged and became one. Love became complete.

Sitting at breakfast the following morning, I glanced up at Jena and told her I had been Karl's wife.

'I was aware of the union,' she said casually.

I should have known I couldn't tell her anything. She saw all.

'I never realised, Jena, that so much love could come from such devastation of another's world.'

'If you mean the child Lootock, then you should know mortality is very high. Fortunately, they are very resilient.'

'They need to be, Jena. Mother knows, life is hard enough for them.'

'Let us put it behind us dear. Karl will be visiting you more often. Does that please you?'

I laughed and said, 'Need you ask!'

My Karl came to visit almost every day. There was an air of tranquillity about the apartment, everything ran smoothly and there were no harsh words. I think my fondest moments were sharing my garden with Karl and talking of my Earth with its soft beauty, birds on the wing and scurrying wildlife. How he laughed at me when I told him there was no better way to see the countryside than on a bicycle.

'You rode an old-fashioned bicycle, Jan? You were brave.'

'They weren't old-fashioned when I was on Earth.'

'Did you ride one of those bicycles with a large wheel and a tiny wheel?'

'Now they really *were* old-fashioned, Karl, even in my time!'

I looked up at the oak tree and asked him if he had ever climbed such a tree.

'I have never climbed any tree, least of all one so large.'

'I wonder sometimes, Karl, if you ever had a childhood. I have climbed trees and known the safety of being cradled in its boughs. The world seemed such a big place when I was small, a place of magic to be explored.'

He just smiled and said, 'I love you, Jan.'

Falo visited one lunchtime and actually sat and drank tea with us. I felt uneasy in her company, although she was very pleasant. She asked Jena if I had coupled with Karl and Jena found great pleasure in telling her all was well. Then Falo brought up the subject of my actions when I visited the Hill Farmers. I was noticeably afraid at this point and decided to leave the table and put some space between Falo and me. Jena stood also and clasped my hand to reassure me.

'I have dealt with the matter of the Hill Farmers, Falo. There is no reason to continue distressing Jan about her behaviour at this point in time, it would be imprudent to cause her anxiety. Jan is carrying her child for Arena!'

'I am?' I said. 'Yes, of course I am ... I'm pregnant.'

Falo grinned at me and said, 'I must congratulate you on the child you were not aware of.'

'Jena loves to surprise me, but she always tells Karl first.' I was gripping Jena's finger like a vice.

'Well done, Jena,' said Falo, 'I shall take my leave of you and follow your progress, Jan.' Then she left.

'Oh Jena, Jena, what are we going to do? Whatever will happen to us now?'

'Calm yourself, Jan. I have cared for you long enough to know when you have conceived. Now take this container into your room and bring me a specimen of your urine.'

I'm glad it wasn't glass, as I dropped it twice. After a moment or two, Jena came into my room. 'Not finished yet, Jan?'

'I can't do it, Jena. I'm so mixed up, the piddle won't come.'

'Just relax, Jan.' She crossed the room and turned the water taps on in the hand basin, then the shower.

'Oh lovely. That's better, Jena. You can turn them off now, I'm doing it.'

She took the container and asked me to follow her into the hospital wing via her living quarters when I was ready. This I did.

'You are with child, Jan, but a blood test will confirm it, dear. Roll up your sleeve.'

'Oh Mother of Arena, that was a close call, Jena! Suppose you had been wrong?'

'I am seldom wrong about such matters, Jan. I know you too well, your personality changes.'

'But I'm still me!'

'Yes of course you are, dear,' she said with a pleasing smile.

When Karl came that evening, I pulled him through the door and waited for Jena to give him the news. She had already done so, because he put his arms around me and whispered, 'Who is a clever girl then?'

Later that week, the door was unlocked from my apartment to the hospital wing as Jena and Nada made full use of it to examine my progress. Perhaps my personality had changed, or

Nada had. There was no animosity between us, as there had been during my other pregnancies. Still, Nada was always short on talk, much preferring to get the job done and go. When she left one afternoon, I mentioned to Jena just how little talking Nada did, almost to the point of being antisocial. Jena laughed at me and told me it was because I was unaware of Nada's telepathy capabilities.

'What's that?' I asked.

'Nada is quite capable of reading people's thoughts. I hardly scratch the surface in that field.'

'Do you mean she knows what I'm thinking?'

'Only if she thinks it is validated.'

'Ooo hell, I had better watch myself!'

Jena seemed to find this all amusing, but I wasn't too happy knowing my thoughts were no longer a secret.

Time passed and my tummy grew bigger. Jena told me I was going to have a little girl. Now to find a name for her. My life became a ritual of living by the clock. Exercises, both breathing and physical, were enforced, then examinations and tests. But at no time could I say I was lonely, with Jena, Nada and her helper Quil around me, all people I liked, although I was never sure about Nada. She lived to work and took it very seriously.

I was slouching in a chair one day, watching Jena and Nada working, when Nada, still with her back to me, suggested I sat properly in the chair to support my back and protect the baby by not crossing my legs. I did her bidding and thought: what a good thing she doesn't see what antics I get up to with Karl!

'No, but Jena does. Perhaps she should be a little more stringent with you.'

I sat wide-eyed as Jena turned, saying, 'Why don't you go and lie on your bed. It is more relaxing, dear.'

'You are too easy, Jena. The girl takes liberties.'

I stood up, ready to do battle with Nada, but all she said was, 'Do as Jena asks, Jan.' She hadn't even turned to look at me, not once, and yet she knew. Uncanny and spooky, that's what I called it.

The weeks passed and life was hectic. I noticed Nada seemed to show concern for Jena's wellbeing and I was worried for Jena, although she made no complaints.

Nada and Quil arrived one morning and I approached Nada, asking her if she could make the time to walk with me in my garden. I think she sensed my feelings and agreed to do so . Once we were alone, I asked her to hear me out before putting me in my place, which is what I expected of her.

'I know Jena is unwell, Nada. If she is putting off treatment until the baby is born, it might make things worse for her. I know you are more than capable of seeing this pregnancy through, so could I ask you to see that Jena is taken care of now, before she gets worse?'

She smiled kindly at me, took my hand and patted it. 'I appreciate your concern for Jena, but you would not settle with another guardian. It would be unwise to put stress on you at this time.'

'Nada, bring whoever you wish, even you if you are not too busy, and I will do whatever you ask of me. Just do what is best for my Jena. Please.'

Her look was one of concern, then she said, 'Leave it with me, Jan. I will not let Jena suffer unnecessarily. Your good intentions are well noted.'

The next day Jena asked me to sit and drink tea with her. I was aware she had something to discuss with me.

'You have two months before the birth, Jan. I am aware of your concern for me, Nada and I had a long discussion on the subject. I am equally concerned for you and I do not feel inclined to pass my duties on to any Arenian who is not familiar with your case or your temperament. Now be truthful with me, Jan, do you think you could bring yourself to obey Nada?'

'You mean, let her take your place until you are well again?'

'Yes, dear. I will have the satisfaction of knowing you will be well cared for providing you can cope with Nada's strict temperament.'

53

I rose from my chair and cuddled her. 'Just ask Nada to keep me informed of your progress and I will do whatever she bids me to. Does that answer your question, Jena?'

The tension went from her, which pleased me. Now my mum could get well, all I had to do was be tolerant with friend Nada. Not an easy task.

That afternoon Jena got ready to leave as Nada familiarized herself with Jena's private apartment. I stayed out of harm's way so that Jena would have no reason to change her mind. She was ready to leave and I could not stop my tears. I didn't attempt to hug her, I just waved from the far end of the room. I was even unable to wish her well, words would not come.

With Jena gone, Nada saw my tears and came to me. I threw my arms around her and begged her to make my Jena well again because I did love my mum. She sat me at the table and brought us refreshments.

'Now drink that, Jan, because I am not having Jena's number one girl upset. Karl will come this evening, so you will not be short of company and as soon as Jena settles she has promised to contact us. Now with all that to look forward to, I think you should dry your eyes to look nice when Karl arrives.'

I looked up at her and thought: she is quite human. She is really working hard to be nice to me.

'Jena will get well, won't she, Nada?'

'Yes, Jan. Hopefully she will be back in time to see your little girl born.'

'That's great, she may even be able to hold her. We are going to get along fine, Nada. You'll see.'

'You would do all this for Jena's peace of mind, Jan?' She looked as mystified at me as I had at her being so kind.

'Jena is the best friend I have ever had. Now it's my turn to be a friend to her.'

'May our Mother smile on you, Jan. I shall.'

Much to my surprise, we grew close. I realised she was bending her ways and conversation to come to my level, but I let her see my appreciation of it. There was the odd occasion when she was preoccupied and her voice was a little starchy, but I would go to great pains to obey her and then tease her that if she was not patient, I would not let her hold baby when she arrived.

I leant against my great oak tree late one afternoon, thinking of my role as a mother. What role? I thought. Nine months of pregnancy, delivery and a couple of weeks seeing her, but only to breast feed her, if permitted. Then she would be taken from me and become a memory that would return like an echo in the nights when sleep did not come, or the days when time stood still and a loneliness captured me. Yes, she would become an echo that would cause me pain. A sweet pain.

'Jan,' called Nada.

'I'm on my way!' I shouted. After all, a promise is a promise and I wasn't going to let Jena down.

'Jena is on the computer. Would you like to speak to her?'

That put me in a better mood, in fact I was bubbling over with excitement. She was really happy to know Nada and I were good friends, which was the way I put it to her. She hoped I was giving lots of thought to a name for the baby. Karl and Virg had visited her and she was going to the rehabilitation centre soon. There was a hurtful silence when the screen went blank. Nada put a friendly arm round my shoulders and told me it wouldn't be long before Jena would be back with us.

I invited her for a walk in my garden before we had dinner. I told her that most families on Earth had a garden and how they spent their leisure hours tending it and sitting in it. Then she surprised me and showed me a box on the wall near the entrance to the garden; when it was unlocked, one could use the controls within to roll the grass back and reveal a swimming pool. When I complained that Jena had never told me, Nada said it was because no one was allowed to swim without a chaperon for safety reasons. Jena would have had to sit beside the pool while it was uncovered.

Life with Nada wasn't bad really.

One week to go for the birth and Jena was back, walking steady and unaided. Every day was like Christmas now. Nada was going to stay until I was in good health after the little one was born. I was becoming quite fidgety. Quil fussed over me and I fussed over Jena. Nada looked on when she was not working and took it all in.

Nada called me to waken one morning. Waking was no problem, but getting up was. For some reason my legs would not work; in fact, I could not feel them. 'Don't worry Jena aboutb it Nada, but I think we have a problem,' I said.

After an examination, Nada and Quil got me onto a trolley and into the hospital wing. Jena came to the head of the trolley and stayed with me.

'Am I paralysed, Jena?'

'Temporarily, yes. But only until we get the baby out. You are not worried, are you, Jan?'

'No,' I lied, 'you will fix it and make it right.'

There was quite a lot of activity, but Jena stayed at my head as together we watched.

'Jena, will Minu be coming?' I asked.

'I do hope not, Jan. With work like this, we find him a hindrance.'

'I'm not going to the dark time then?'

'No, my dear, if we turn baby and deliver her, your feeling will return again.'

'What are we waiting for then? Let's go!'

Jena grinned, 'Impatient even at a time like this! What am I going to do with you?'

Nada and Quil moved to the other side of the room, so I whispered to Jena, 'I'm frightened.'

'I know, Jan. I promise you it will be over soon without too much discomfort.' Then she held my hand.

Nada came to me putting a mask over my face. 'Jena, can you control her while Quil and I work?'

Jena nodded while Quil strapped my wrists. By this time I felt I hadn't a care in the world. Someone seemed to be pushing my body, but it didn't matter. I grew very hot and tired as though I had run a race and lost. It was all too much, and I think I fell asleep.

I was awakened by someone mopping my face and neck. I

tried to talk but nothing happened. Jena moistened my lips and I managed a 'Thank you.'

'Oh you are with us, Jan.'

'That was Nada,' I said.

'She is not quite with us yet, Nada.'

I looked at Jena trying to make me comfortable. 'Is that better, dear?'

'Mmm.'

'Do you want to see your little girl?'

'No.' I closed my eyes and forgot the world and its problems.

When I eventually awoke, Quil and Jena were drinking tea while Nada was checking the baby.

'You wouldn't have a spare cup of that brew for me, would you, Quil?'

All beaming with smiles, they came to me and Nada placed the child beside me. She automatically unwrapped her, knowing I liked to inspect my children, then she wrapped her again. Her little body still had the wrinkles on it from the time it had spent within me. She was perfect.

'Have you given any thought to a name for her?' asked Jena.

'Echo. I shall call her Echo.'

'Why Echo?' asked Nada.

'It's just a pretty name,' I answered.

It was accepted and after a few days she was taken by the Arenians. My milk was dried up and life resumed at its normal pace as the hospital wing was closed. Nada and Quil disappeared to take on duties of a similar nature elsewhere within Arena. Echo was just another page in my log-book. Dear little Echo.

CHAPTER SEVEN
TRAUMATIC

One day Jena announced: 'I think you have earned a holiday, Jan. Would you like three weeks with Asta as a companion?'

'Asta makes me laugh, she's great company. Yes please, I'd like that.'

It was all arranged that a guard take me to the rehabilitation centre, where I would meet Asta. She greeted me warmly. I went through the usual process of doctors, then Asta took me to my room, giving me a key card, telling me that I was quite free to do as I wished as long as I informed her where I was going.

'The red lounge,' I said.

'Where?'

'To the lounge where Arenians sit and listen to music through earphones. That's my favourite place, Asta.'

'I thought we might go to dinner together.'

I capitulated and within fifteen minutes we were in the restaurant being served by the very polite Arenian waiters and waitresses.

'Do you remember telling me the waiters were robots?' I reminded her.

'Do you remember believing me?' she laughed. 'But it cured you of your fear of them at the time.'

I couldn't argue with that. She had taken my fear of them away.

I ate heartily, but left myself with a terrible thirst from eating caviar, so I sat at the table sipping juice. Asta motioned to a male Arenian to join us. She introduced him as Ramm, a guard also on leave. They talked of what they were going to do and where they would go, mostly on the surface. I casually looked about the restaurant and noticed a dark-skinned, plump lady sitting alone. She looked the epitome of loneliness, so much so that I felt a sadness for her. I asked Asta if I could invite her to our table, to which she replied, 'Not a good idea, Jan.'

'May I join her at her table then?'

'I said, not a good idea, Jan.'

I looked questioningly at her, unable to fathom her out.

'She belongs to the Amazons. Keep clear of her, Jan.'

I said no more on the subject, but wondered a great deal.

When we returned to our room Asta asked if I would care to go on a hopper with her and Ramm in the morning. I told her I wasn't keen on visiting the surface, but I would agree to go just this once. We retired at a respectable hour to ensure we made an early start.

Next morning we arrived on the surface wearing surface clothing and were taken in little runabout trucks to the waiting hoppers. (I still think of them as flying bedsteads.) We took off in a vertical take off as I held tight to my seat. Asta laughed at me and winked. 'All right, Jan?'

I nodded but didn't let go. The hopper seated four and a pilot, so we had a spare seat. Ramm spread himself over two seats and remarked, 'What a nice way to travel.' He seemed a cheerful man, and I was glad he'd come with us.

The little hopper sped across the rock-strewn surface with the pilot continually talking to base. He hadn't mentioned seeing any Stone men, which pleased me.

'On the port side,' said the pilot, 'there is a herd of wildebeest.'

I watched them stampeding, sending the dusty ground up like a smouldering forest fire. I saw no robots herding them. It brought back memories of the time I had escaped and was herded to a slaughter station. I was already wishing I hadn't come on this trip.

'There is a drink and sandwiches beneath your seats for those of you who had no breakfast,' the pilot told us.

Asta thanked him and told him, perhaps later.

'There is a lake ahead, would you like to stretch your legs for fifteen minutes?'

Ramm was all in favour of that, so we landed.

The pilot told us he was unfamiliar with the area and had only been piloting in these parts for a week. He suggested we did not go too close to the water's edge in case there were crocodiles. I didn't need telling twice; I hated crocs. I didn't even walk about much, in case of snakes. I was keen to get airborne again. It was strange: if I had been a trooper and armed to the teeth, this fear would not have prevailed. There was a strength with my troop, a need for us all to watch over each other. I missed them.

The craft was airborne again. I was pleased to be looking at the view from a great height. Suddenly we seemed to be in shadow and the engines faltered. 'We have been struck by a flock of birds,' called the pilot. 'Fasten your seatbelts!'

The craft was pirouetting and plunging earthward. Ramm had been occupying two seats, so he was having difficulty sorting himself out. It was too late; the hopper crashed. There was silence as I lay on my side, still strapped to my seat. I didn't feel any pain, just discomfort at my predicament.

'Asta, Asta, are you all right?'

'I think so, Jan, but I cannot move.'

After what seemed an age, I untangled myself and crawled to Asta, helping her untangle her legs and seatbelt. She had blood on the leg of her slacks but she shrugged it off, telling me to get the others out. Ramm's neck was broken, one didn't have to touch him to know. His body was twisted badly. A moan from the pilot told us we had to get him out quickly. The glass dome was not broken as the hopper lay on its side, which meant climbing out of a side door that was above us. The pilot struggled but was unable to move without help. As we freed him, he gave instructions to Asta, telling her to activate the strobe beacon and switch on the intercom. The intercom did not work.

Together we pushed him out the door above us, then Asta and I collected medical equipment, food and water. Our next

60

move was to get to the rocks for cover. The pilot had not seen any Stone men, so we hoped they were not in the vicinity. The sun was high and its rays almost deadened one's senses as we huddled between rocks trying to sort ourselves out. The blood on Asta must have come from Ramm; thankfully she and I were unharmed save for the odd bruising. The pilot had a bad gash in his leg and a broken arm, both of which Asta treated to make him comfortable. Now to wait.

The sun had sapped our remaining strength. We awaited nightfall and the cold that would sweep the land. With the setting of the sun we could see the strobe lights more clearly, which meant the Stone men could too. Asta laid out the equipment we might need as night approached: a torch, flare gun, knife and hip laser. We each had something to eat, then we settled down for a long night.

Twice through that night, Asta attended to the pilot, whose name was Otto. He complained of being in pain and was not looking good at all. His leg needed stitches, but Asta could only bind it and hope the bleeding would stop. It was the first time on the surface at night that there was no red glow. It actually grew dark with a sky of black velvet embroidered with jewels and a bright full moon: the very same moon that Jim and I, on Earth of 1970, had gazed at in wonder. Now it shone down on me in this hostile land as I waited the night through. There was movement among the rocks that caused us to hold our breaths a few times, but Asta thought it was wildlife of the crawly kind. Needless to say, sleep was taken as cat-naps.

The indigo sky changed to soft blue before the sun dazzled our eyes and crept over the rocks to torture our bodies and dull our senses. Thanks to Asta, Otto was now reasonably well. He assumed that this would be the time of day that all scout transport would be out looking for us, making it imperative that we did not leave the crash site.

'Do either of you have an implant for them to track?' asked Otto.

'No,' said Asta, 'Jan had one but it was removed on her return from Earth.'

'I am not sure if the hopper's tracker is working.'

'We should know soon,' said Asta.

We sipped at our water ration and ate what was left of the broken sandwiches. Asta gave us a salt tablet from the first aid box she had salvaged. She had done well in such an emergency. Certainly Otto was in no position to run things.

My heart almost stopped as I looked at the shattered craft and saw a dozen Stone men heading towards us. I alerted Asta and Otto, then we lay low in silence. It was only then I hoped we hadn't left any tracks.

On reaching the craft, they set about ransacking it. Ramm's body was dragged from the wreckage and dismembered. I crouched on all fours and held my hands over my head and ears. We had to keep silent, which was no easy task as I wept. Asta's hand stroked my head. How, in the name of all that is holy, could one human do that to another? I thought. Asta pulled my hand away from my ear and whispered, 'They are making camp, Jan. They will be here for some time, so try to control yourself.'

Pressing my hands over my eyes, I tried to stop my tears. I could not look between the rocks for fear of giving our position away if I saw something grotesque. As if we had not suffered enough, a damned snake wriggled from under a rock. Now we were all in danger of being bitten. Asta was marvellous. She slipped her jacket off, wrapping it round her arm, then with a knife in her wrapped hand, she sliced it across the snake's neck. It was as well she had covered her hand, as one of its fangs had hooked into her jacket. The snake dispensed with, Asta donned her jacket and tended to Otto as though nothing had happened. She hadn't made a sound. May our Mother bless her!

There was a humming sound. Asta motioned me to stay low. Otto whispered, 'Chariots.' Then we heard the explosions of hand bombs. Only Asta watched between the rocks. When she was satisfied that all Stonies were dead, she fired the flare gun. The chariots, all three of them, circled us for ten minutes until a larger craft arrived. It landed amidst clouds of dust, but far enough away to spare us that discomfort. Troopers scrambled from the craft, checking the crashed hopper and helping us aboard. I don't think it took five minutes to have us out of there.

We were all hospitalised. I couldn't wait to see Jena, who I knew would visit me. As she entered the door, I opened my arms and with a beaming smile we embraced each other. In two minutes flat, I had told her everything, emphasising Asta's care, leadership and bravery. I could not praise her enough. My fun-loving Arenian had turned out to be a very level-headed heroine.

'Can I come home now, Mum?'

'The hospital will not release you today. Perhaps tomorrow.'

'I don't want to go to the surface any more.'

'Then stay within Arena and enjoy yourself. You really do need a holiday, more so now.'

'Jena,' I said in a serious whisper, 'they ate the Arenian Ramm.'

'Yes, dear. Thanks be to the power and our Lady Mother, he felt nothing. He was more fortunate than some have been. Better you stay here, Jan, and let the nursing staff help you through such a traumatic experience. I shall have them contact Minu. He is your personal physician for trauma.'

'Are you managing all right alone, Jena?'

She grinned and ruffled my hair, 'I am managing very well, Jan, but it is too quiet without you. Yes, my dear, I do miss you. Now do as you are told and have a restful holiday. Goodbye, my dear.' Then she did something that I had only ever done to her: she pulled me towards her and kissed my head. Then she left, as I stared at the closed door behind her. She really was my mum now, because she loved and missed me. I was so lucky.

Asta and I were discharged from the hospital, but Minu ordered me to be back in my room by ten o'clock each night. I did get to sit in that beautiful red room that I found so restful. I was like the elderly Arenians: earphones, eyes closed and contented to sit and take it all in.

Asta suggested we see a play. I wasn't going to refuse her anything after the way she had taken care of me. We readied ourselves and went to the theatre. It was the same hall to which Ross had taken me in my former life, when we saw a choir of young Arenians who had sung to me. An Arenian came onto the stage and told us what the play was called, who wrote it and so forth. I wasn't in the least bit interested. I just wanted to see the play.

'Arenians, I leave you with *Leon*.' Then he walked off the stage.

A man rose from a seat in the audience with a spotlight on him and walked towards the stage, passing through people and chairs as though they were not there. I went cold with fear and screamed, '*A ghost!*' as I tried to climb over the seats in the opposite direction. Someone grabbed me and I felt a pain at the back of my neck. Everything went black. Even in the blackness I saw that ghost and was grateful when someone awakened me. I threw my arms around them for protection. A guard in his black uniform unclasped my arms from his neck as Asta, with the aid of another man, tried to calm me. Fortunately, they had got me out of the theatre. I was bustled into a runaround car and taken back to the hospital where some rotter jabbed a needle into me. I awoke in bed once more with Minu at my side.

Seating himself on the side of my bed, he questioned me. I wouldn't answer him except to cuss about being strapped down.

'If you will stay quiet for just a moment, I will take the restraints from you.' He was as good as his word, taking his time while telling me that if I did not lie quietly, they would be put on again.

'I won't struggle, Minu. There isn't any ghost here.'

After telling him of the apparition I had seen walking through people and seats, he told me that it was a hologram.

'No, Minu, it was a man.'

'A hologram is what we use as you used cameras on Earth to show films. It is 'holo', with no substance. Rather like a beam of light. It cannot harm you, dear.'

I looked at him suspiciously, but he only patted my hand and asked me to be patient for a few moments as he left my bedside. He was replaced by a nurse. She never spoke. She just made herself busy straightening the bed.

Minu returned with a box, seating himself back on the bed. 'Computers, Jan. You like computers. How about a talking computer, would you like to see one work? It is only a dictionary.'

'I had one, Minu, but it broke.'

'I heard about that old tin box you had. It was old-fashioned and not very good. This one is a little more up-to-date and has a picture hologram to talk to.'

I stared at him and the box. 'A hologram in a box?'

He explained that it could only work within the box, because the box had lenses and reflectors built into it. Then he called two nurses to help him fit it up. That was a sham. They only stood by me while he opened the box. The lid didn't lift off, it extended upwards on slides like a roof. He flicked a switch on the box as the inside glowed like a phosphorus light. 'Now I shall ask it a question, or perhaps you would like to ask it, Jan. Remember, it is only a modern dictionary.'

I shook my head.

Minu spoke to it. 'Computer, what is history?'

The thing came to life in the form of a face between the lid and the rim of the box, a face I could see through. I grabbed a nurse, who was already holding me. The head spoke: 'A continuous record of important events. A study of past events. The course of human affairs. A systematic account of natural phenomena. Historical ...' Minu switched it off and the face disappeared.

I was still clutching the nurse tightly.

'Now that was a hologram, Jan. Nothing to be afraid of, my dear, was it?'

My gaze was still fixed on the box. He rested it on the bed and stood up.

'I don't think I would like a computer with a hologram, Minu. It's unnatural and spooky.'

He laughed and told me to sleep the night in the hospital and if I felt well enough, I could resume my holiday tomorrow. Which I did.

After a few days, I was taken to my room by Asta and told our holiday had come to an end.

'Well that was short lived, Asta. Since when does eight days constitute three weeks?'

'Since the council has ordered all leave to be cancelled and has requisitioned the facilities. They will be used for Arenians who must be moved here for safety.'

'What are you saying, Asta, are we at war?'

'Only with a volcano that is due to erupt very soon. Arenians in that vicinity must be moved, so they are coming to live here until it is safe to return home.'

So home we journeyed and I wasn't sorry. That holiday had been traumatic.

CHAPTER EIGHT
VOLCANO

Jena greeted me on my return home. It felt good being back.
'I've got news, Jena. A volcano is due to erupt very soon.'
'Next month to be precise, Jan.'
'Oh I thought it would be sooner. Is it near here?'
'No, we are quite safe. You will notice there has been a door fitted to your bedroom, the Arenian Njee will be using it. You will be sleeping in the hospital wing with five other Arenians. Two showers have been installed in there and two toilets. I think you will all manage if you can respect each other's needs. How do you feel about having five sisters, Jan?'
I just looked about me in bewilderment. 'Five?'
She brought two teas and sat at the table. I joined her, still feeling numb.
'You do enjoy family life, I hope. They need somewhere to live until the danger has passed. Many Arenians are in the same position as us.'
'If they knew about the volcano, then why did they let people live there?'
'Because it was dormant. It came as a surprise to us when we were told it would awaken. It will be quite violent when it does erupt, catastrophic enough for our descendants to return and ensure our safety.'
I couldn't have heard her right. Descendants? Returning?
'What descendants are you talking about, Jena?'
'Our future, Jan. They can return to our time, but we must not go forward to their time.'
I had heard her right! No. No, it wasn't possible. Or was it? My children's children ... 'The future, Jena?'
'Yes, Jan.'
'How? I mean when, what year? You do mean Arenians,

don't you? How do they get here? It's too much, Jena, just let me think for a minute. No, tell me again.'

'Just as we can return to Earth of your time, so our descendants can return to our time. After all, Jan, if we can travel in time, they must also be able to.'

'Hell, Jena, I've only just got used to living in the future; now you land me with another bombshell! Where does it all end?'

She laughed at my confusion and said, 'Just drink your tea, Jan.'

By heck, talk about scrambling your brains! Arena never ceased to amaze me, but this really left me gobsmacked.

I slept the night in the hospital wing. Little portable dividers were placed at the side of each bed for privacy. I felt very alone in there and wondered if Jena's scanner was watching over me. This was one time I hoped it was, if only for company's sake.

By twelve noon the next day, the Arenian Njee arrived and told Jena her three wards would be arriving at five-thirty that evening. She was concerned about her computer chip records, which she was unable to bring with her. She need not have worried, as they came an hour later. Jena showed her the apartment, but they spent most of their time in Jena's workplace and quarters. I was asked to bring them tea, which they drank in our living room.

'I am Njee, Jan. You will be meeting my wards this evening - Fran, Anja and Judi. I hope you will try as hard to be amicable with them as they have been instructed to be with you.'

'Are they all Arenians, Njee?' I asked.

'Of course they are.'

'Then, Njee, you have nothing to fear. We will get on fine.'

Jena put a friendly hand on my shoulder and said, 'Jan was only born on Earth, her loyalties are with Arena.'

Njee said no more to me, but I couldn't help wonder what the young Arenians were like if they had to be ordered to be respectful. I didn't have long to wait. At five-thirty on the dot they began to arrive. We were introduced, then Njee showed them their sleeping quarters. I sat in the living room and hung my head low as I tried to suppress a smile at overhearing Njee lecture her three wards. It was unbelievable. 'You will mix with the Earthling as little as possible. They are known for their bad temperament and can be violent creatures. Do not give her the opportunity to challenge you. Now go into dinner as soon as you have readied yourselves.'

I sat at the table awaiting them. Fancy us little Earthlings having such a reputation! I had to suppress a giggle as I thought: should I ask Jena for a bottle of blood to help wash down the last Arenian I ate? No! I'll show them! I'll let them see I'm as human or more so than they are. We all sat in silence save for Jena and Njee. The girls hardly looked up from their plates. Poor buggers, they probably thought I was going to throw my dinner plate at them any moment. I would have to ask Jena to educate Njee. Perhaps I was the first Earthling she'd met.

'Fran,' said Njee, 'will you clear the table?'

I butted in. 'You ladies have been at work all day. I shall be glad to make that my task.'

Njee waved Fran aside and thanked me.

'That's all right Njee. It's the least I can do for my new sisters.' Then I joyfully tidied the table. As I walked past a smiling Jena, I winked.

We all sat to let our meal go down. The silence was almost unbearable, so I started. 'Well now, who is going first?' They sat in amazement with our elders looking on. 'Come on, girls, tell me what you do all day. You first, Fran, I'm dying to know. I had a house sister once, I miss her terribly. Now I have got five sisters; how lucky can a person get? Well, Fran?'

I lapped it up. Three young Arenians, all older than me, on their best behaviour telling me all about their work. I felt great and I hadn't attempted to devour any of them yet. Oh boy!

Fran, the eldest at twenty-three, was going to be a robotics engineer. Anja, twenty, was studying for a degree in horticulture and twenty-one-year-old Judi was training to be a sea shepherd.

'I have all my qualifications in here,' I said patting my tummy, 'I reproduce for our Mother.'

Then they came out of their shells and began to ask how many children I had produced and all about them. It was a joy seeing them come to life. I wandered over to Jena and, taking her hand, I led her into the garden. I told her what I had overheard, then I asked if she could tell Njee that not all Earthians are bad. Jena looked very seriously at me and said, 'Most Arenians have only seen or heard about Earthians on the viewing screen, usually because of their violent outbreaks in the militant camps. I shall not inform Njee to the contrary. I shall let her learn from you, Jan. I think you are doing exceptionally well on your own. It has taken three lives for you to mature, and I am very proud of you.'

'Do you think it might have something to do with that Arenian I call Mum? Eh, Mum?'

She smiled and together we returned to the living room. The girls had started their hour of study before relaxation, so I watched the viewer using earphones to ensure I did not disturb them. I lost the use of my computer to fill in my log-book so it had to be written by hand. I couldn't complain, the Arenians had the same problem.

It was two days later when the other Arenians joined us, Acta and Myer. Acta was in training to become a trooper, Myer was already a trooper. They were twenty-two years old. Jena was their temporary guardian. As it happened, we got on pretty well. I stayed clear of them in the mornings to give them a chance to use all the facilities to get ready for work. I was glad I didn't have to compete with them; I was slow to waken and liked to take my time to come around to meet the day. Fran was my favourite. She occasionally put us in our place if discussions looked like becoming arguments. She also had a gentleness and understanding. I felt she would have made an excellent guardian as she had a mum's qualities. I never felt that way about Njee.

I loved the evenings when the girls talked of their day and their laughter at mishaps and so forth. I was never left out of anything. I could always call to mind my own mishaps when I was a trooper. They thought it hilarious when I told them the first time I sat on a bidet, thinking it to be a toilet, and my surprise when I thought someone had pulled the chain on me. Even that caused laughter when I had to explain what a toilet chain was, for they had nothing as old-fashioned as toilet chains.

Weekends, the pool was unlocked. Jena or Njee sat by the pool while we swam in our birthday suits. Acta and Myer were always in trouble when swimming. Their competitiveness was a danger to anyone near them. It seemed to be win or die with them, but they would never hurt anyone knowingly.

One weekend Jena was sitting in a chair at the entrance of the garden, so I squatted on the floor beside her, complaining that I didn't get to see Karl now that the girls were here. She told me that if I was in need of his company, she would give it her attention. That was good enough for me and I thanked her.

After the girls went off to work the following morning, Karl arrived and asked if I was ready to leave.

'I am not going to the surface, Karl, and certainly not to see those half-grown turds called Hill Farmers.'

'Perhaps you would like me to take you to my apartment, which is where I intended to take you.'

'Well why didn't you say so? Come on, let's go!'

Jena told Karl to make sure I returned home no later than five thirty. Then we left.

I was most surprised to see Karl's apartment for the first time. It was very much a male environment, especially with the weights and exercise machines. I was also surprised and delighted to see a photograph of me on the wall. It seemed to turn and move depending on what direction one viewed it from.

'Now I know you have other wives, Karl. You hung that photo there just to impress me, didn't you?'

Wrapping his arms about me he whispered, 'I do not have to impress the only lady who loves me enough to become my wife.'

I didn't and couldn't answer him. His lips sealed to mine and as our bodies began to writhe, my only thoughts were of

71

the pleasures of the moment with a man I would sell my soul for. Talk was a forgotten art while my senses responded to his every licentious act.

I was reluctant to return home that afternoon: why must pleasure end? I was eager for more of this bronze God of love.

Jena asked Karl if he wished to stay for dinner. I was glad he refused, as I didn't want to share him with the girls. I watched the viewer that evening, only half interested in it. The girls were using the pool when one of them suggested that the trees and flowers be removed to make a ball court. I was out of my seat like a shot. 'Don't you dare touch one of those plants, or I'll make you wish you had never been born!'

Myer remarked that they were not real and it would only be temporary, just until they moved out.

No one was going to touch my beautiful garden, so I went to Jena's office, barged in and said, 'The answer's no. That's the end of it.'

'I have not the slightest idea of what you are talking about, Jan, but before we sort it out, you know better than to enter my office without asking. Is that clear? Now you may tell me what is upsetting you.'

'They want to uproot my garden to make room for a ball court. I won't have it, Jena. I don't mind them using it, but I will not have it torn up. I won't!'

'Quite correct, Jan. It remains and they will treat it with the same respect that you show it. That is final!'

That was the answer I had hoped for. I let the matter drop, knowing Jena always kept her word. My garden was safe.

As I left the office, Njee and the girls stood watching me. I realised my ranting was all very new to them. No Arenian subordinate shouts at a superior. I walked towards Njee, who gave the impression she was ready to stand and defend herself. 'I've had my little shout for the day and that's an end to it,' I said. 'Now we can get on with our lives.'

There was a silence as I returned to the viewer. As I sat down, the girls returned to their activities. I grinned and thought: well, I don't have to eat Njee for supper tonight. I wondered what she really thought of me.

Each day, as the girls went to work, so Karl called for me. Life was one big enjoyable session of lovemaking. On the whole, I got on pretty well with the girls. Njee had very little to say to me, although there was not a lot she missed.

Falo came one evening. The girls sat quietly as they listened to her questions. She glanced at a couple of log-books and then returned them. I stayed at the far end of the room.

'How are you getting along with so many young Arenians, Jan?' she asked.

Sod it. I had been hoping she hadn't noticed me. 'They are my sisters, Falo. I think it's great.'

She stared at me for a long moment as though she enjoyed my apprehension of her, then she turned to Acta. 'It has come to my attention that you chose to have a confrontation in the field with a fellow trooper. What have you to say, Acta?'

'I thought my argument was validated, Falo.'

'But you saw fit to continue that argument after your leader forbade you?'

'I thought I was right, Falo.'

'I am displeased with you, Acta. You will apologise in front of your fellow troopers in the morning and beg their forgiveness.'

'But, Falo, if you knew the reason for my questioning of the situation, then I am sure that you would see that I was in the right.'

'Now you question my right!' snarled Falo as she touched the side of her leg that pocketed her punishment stick. I could see where this was leading and I was mightily worried. The rest of us stood almost dumbstruck at the situation, with neither of them backing down. I thought that Njee would have tried to defuse the tension, but she stayed silent. Jena, however, thought differently and told Acta to be silent and heed Falo. That at least should have given Acta time to review her situation and assess her position. Hopefully Falo would feel less hurt by Acta's forcefulness. It was not to be. Acta politely but firmly stood her ground and Falo was left to enforce her rank. The stun stick was drawn from her leg pocket as the young Arenians slowly backed away, but not Acta. It was more than I could bear.

'No, Falo!' I yelled. 'Acta is my sister, you will not hurt her.'

Falo's eyes met mine and I saw fury in them. She touched Acta with the stick as Acta's body jerked backwards and slumped to the floor. I was at Acta's side in a flash and telling Falo that she would have to pass me if she wanted to hurt any more of my sisters. Njee knelt beside me and, with a pain in my neck, blackness came. All was silent.

I awoke on my bed in the hospital wing with Fran beside me. 'What happened, Fran?'

Fran called Jena, who explained that Njee had rendered me unconscious to prevent Falo using the stunner on me.

'What about Acta?' I asked.

'Njee is with her now. Falo punished her as she did you when you were a trooper. She is resting in bed.'

'Do you have something for a bad headache, Jena? Then I will get up.'

She helped me to rise and took me into the living room. Everyone fell silent as I entered. As Jena seated me to get something to relieve the pain, the girls gathered around me and thanked me for trying to help Acta. I didn't say a word, I just wondered why they hadn't backed me up. As Jena explained to me later, it would have turned bad for them and been put on their records. They were taught obedience from a very young age. It would have broken a rule which had been embedded in them. From that day on the girls treated me like a queen and Njee treated me like one of her girls.

'Bed time, ladies,' came Jena's voice.

'Already?' I complained. 'Fran never goes to bed as early as us.'

'Fran is older,' replied Jena with a flashing grin, then added, 'And you are with child.'

My sisters hugged and congratulated me as though I had performed a miracle. I had, from their point of view. They hadn't even carried their own clone yet, and here was I, younger than them, expecting my second child for my host Claire. Njee gave me an Arenian arm shake and sincerely congratulated me. I felt tall.

My trips to Karl's apartment began to slacken off, which never pleased me. Still, someone always had to pass on such news and it always fell to Jena. Poor Jena. Never mind, she always knew I regretted my tussles with her and we remained friends. I think sometimes Njee didn't know whether to laugh or cry at the way I carried on at times. She was not cut out to handle Earthlings. Njee tried to stay clear of me when Nada had to attend me. It had got to the stage now where I was afraid to think of anything bad for fear of Nada picking up on my thoughts.

I happened to be watching Njee working one day and thinking: however would she cope if her three Arenian wards were Earthlings? She would go nuts.

Nada turned and said, 'Never prejudge a fellow being. They may surprise you, Jan.'

I smiled at her, raised my eyebrows and nodded in agreement. Hell, you couldn't even wipe your bottom without an Arenian knowing about it!

'Quite correct!' said Nada in answer to my thoughts. I went and told my oak tree all my secrets. It didn't repeat them.

The girls arrived home and still I was in my garden sitting beneath the oak, telling it the odd thought. In fact I was saying that I couldn't remember what my husband Jim on Earth looked like. I had forgotten. 'How could I forget someone who meant so much to me?' I sighed. 'I wish you could answer some of these questions, my old friend.'

'Who are talking to, Jan?' asked Fran.

'Oh hello, Fran, had a good day?'

'Yes thank you, Jan. Who were you talking to?'

'My old tree, I often talk to it.'

'It is not real, Jan. Don't you think it might be wiser to talk to Jena?' she said, looking concerned.

'The tree is as real as I want it to be and Jena has heard all my complaints many times. The tree suits my mood.'

Fran looked puzzled as she sat down beside me. It was so silent that Fran touched my arm and asked if I was well. I grinned at her and asked her to press the switch on the wall. She did, and the birds sang in my garden. She sat down again and listened with me. She asked me what was so special about a lot of twittering bird sounds.

'Because each bird has its own song of love and love covers so many things. A fading memory, an unborn child destined to fade also. It is never-ending, but I would not be without it.'

She arose, took my hand to help me to rise. 'Dinner must be ready, Jan. Would you honour me by reading a few excerpts from your log-book to me this evening? I would like to know more of these things you speak of.'

I couldn't answer her; I wasn't sure if Jena would permit it.

Jena gave her permission for me to read to Fran. Then the questions started. She wanted to know about the war I had been in, and what had started it. Hell's bells, I was only a kid myself. I told her the Boogie man of the war was Hitler. We blamed him for everything that was wrong or bad. He was the stuff that nightmares were made of for kids. By the time I had finished, Fran hated Hitler as much as I did, especially as he had killed Claire's family.

Jena told us we could stay up a little longer that evening. She had a film of the volcano and asked if we would care to see it. Njee said we should see it as part of our education. Jena inserted the chip as we watched the fury of our world spit at the heavens time and time again in a futile attempt to conquer all. It spewed its red venom over the land and stood tall as a mountain where once only a mound had been. It built its own grave for all to see and stood silent with no heart. Only steam drifted out of the monster, its life spent. My sisters sat in a trance-like state, a look of devastation in their eyes. Nature, the creator of all things, a destroyer of souls.

The film over, there was no sound as I watched them disappear into the hospital wing. I glanced at Jena and Njee. 'My sisters are hurting,' I told them.

'It is a part of growing up, Jan. Now go to bed.'

Sleep didn't come easy that night. I was aware of the restlessness of the others. Jena and Njee came in to check on us; I was surprised how many of us were unable to sleep. A cup of drink was offered to all who could not sleep and as my head touched the pillow, I was in the land of nod.

Five months the girls were with us and in that time we grew close. I felt life was a rich commodity that offered friendship at its every waking day. I was so fortunate.

Soon it was the girls' last day, but because of our cramped conditions, the girls had never been able to have friends to visit them, so Njee and Jena gave them the freedom of what little room we had to do as they wished. The swimming pool was locked and the garden lights put on, making it look like a summer's day. The furniture was pushed back to the wall. The girls had kept pretty quiet about their plans, if indeed they had any. I certainly knew nothing.

Being a Saturday the girls had no work to go to and they all did their own thing. It was all very quiet. Njee was in the office with Jena. It was, in all, a pretty easy come, easy go day.

At noon the door alarm sounded and Jena asked via the intercom who was calling.

'Activate your viewer,' said a male voice.

Jena grinned, but did not do as she was bid. She activated her belt lock. Virg and Karl came in. 'Do not be angry at our unannounced arrival, Jena,' said Virg. 'The girls invited us.'

Jena glanced at Fran. 'You can explain this?' she asked.

'We asked Nada who you preferred to spend your time with and her reply was that Jan preferred Karl and you spend a lot of your holiday in the company of Virg, so we invited them as a thank you for being so kind to us. Njee's visitor has yet to arrive.'

'Who might that be?' asked Njee.

'Wait and see,' answered Fran teasingly.

The men greeted the girls, then Virg sat Jena and Njee down and demanded the girls wait on them with food and wine. Acta and Myer were pleasantly surprised to see a troop leader letting his hair down, so to speak.

77

The door alarm sounded once more and Jena arose to do the honours again. The visitor announced herself as Njee Two Two. Njee's face lit up and said, 'It is my clone sister. Did Nada tell you of her also?'

The girls smiled as Njee vigorously shook her sister's arm. Karl and I stood at the entrance of the garden. With him beside me, it was like being in a wonderland. All the people I loved were happy, but none as happy as I.

The evening passed with much laughter and song. Jena had been bullied by Virg to get her guitar and play for us. Some of the girls danced to the modern music of their day. It was always a mixture of Greek and Cossack dancing. They stood back in wonderment when Karl and I stood close and swayed to a gentle tune played by Jena. I was four and a half months pregnant, that pace was enough for me. Virg had reached above the door and turned the air flow up, or I think we would have melted. Nada had even arranged for extra food to be allotted; she had thought of everything. I made a mental note to thank her when she next visited me.

Time was passing and our guests had to leave, much to our regret. The ladies bid our guests goodbye as I held tight to my Karl. Virg slipped his arms about me and asked if he could visit again soon. He touched my tummy and told me to take great care of the little one, then he stepped back for me to bid Karl goodbye. Jena reminded us that we had an audience. With a blush I whispered good night to Karl. They were gone.

Two of my sisters came to me and asked if Virg had sired any of my children. I frowned and told them no.

'We thought he seemed very concerned at you being with child.'

I laughed, telling them it wasn't uncommon for an Earthling to die in childbirth. It had happened to me in my last life. Virg and I loved each other like brother and sister, and it was his way of saying he cared for me. Their eyes searched mine. I realised they could not comprehend the feelings I spoke of. I tried to explain. 'If anyone ever hurt either of you as Falo did, I would want to kill that person. I love you all as my family.'

One of them gave me her arm to shake. Another touched my hand.

'You are the first Earthian we have met,' said Anja, 'but not at all like we have been told.'

'As my Jena says, it's all part of growing up.'

I couldn't exactly say the apartment was dead without my sisters, but Nada was doing a pretty good job of making it look like a hospital. The evenings were the time I missed them most. Jena and I sat at the dinner table one evening when the girls had been gone a week.

'Lonely?' asked Jena.

'Just a little. Do you find you miss Njee?'

She leaned back in her chair and reminded me that I never had my full three weeks' holiday.

'Are you suggesting I finish it now with this lump in my tummy?'

'If that is what you want, then yes. Nada can treat you just as well in the recreational hospital as she can here.'

'No, I'd much rather have you with me when they play doctors. You do at least tell me what's happening. Why don't you come too? You could do with a rest after taking care of a large family.'

She thought for a while then clasped her hands together. 'Yes, Jan, let us do it. I shall inform Nada of my plans, and hopefully we can journey tomorrow. Of course, Jan, you realise Karl will not be with you, so do not expect Ross to take his place.'

'Oh, Jena, sex isn't the begin all and end all of everything, it's just nice when I can get it.'

'You are a terrible child, Jan, but rest we shall.'

Great, I thought, me and my mum on holiday together. We'd never done that before. I'd try and make it really pleasurable for her.

No sooner the thought than the deed. The following day at noon we were off to the recreational centre. I didn't have to go through the unpleasantries of examinations; instead, we went straight to the hospital where it was agreed I would make myself available every day at a given time. Other than that, I was free. My room was next to Jena's, where we could meet at the end of each day and she would know that I was well. I liked it more and more. I was given a wrist band to wear, which I had to activate if I needed help. It was fitted with a tracking device so that I could always be found.

I ate in the restaurant and enjoyed watching the young Arenians waiting on tables and acknowledging people coming and going. It was a bright clean friendly atmosphere, much better than going to the surface. I had promised Jena that I would not venture to the surface in my condition and she trusted me to keep my word. I hated the surface at the best of times.

I made use of the lounge with its warm glow and friendly quiet atmosphere, one of my favourite places. I noticed the plump coloured lady there whom Asta had told me belonged to the Amazons. I think she recognised me, but neither of us acknowledged each other.

I walked the corridors at a leisurely pace and felt at peace with the world. No cares or worries, not even a yearning for Karl's company. This time belonged to me alone.

A figure stood like a statue at the end of the corridor, with legs astride and hands on hips. I continued walking towards it. Then a voice rang out, 'Run, Earthling.' Only then did I realise it was an Amazon. I was so contented with my surroundings that the abruptness of being challenged did not sink in.

'Why should I run from you, Amazon? I am Arenian. Surely we are friends?' I continued to approach her. I was within three yards of her before I stopped. 'Why should I run from you, Amazon? I couldn't if I wanted to, I am with child.'

I had no fear of her, I knew I had done no wrong, so what was there to fear? She scanned the corridor and gently pushed me back to the wall.

'Do you carry a clone?'

'No, an Arenian child.'

'You may die this day, Earthling. Two male Earthians are loose and I hunt them.'

Now I was afraid. 'Tell me what to do, Amazon. My guardian gave me a wrist band to activate if I need help. Should I do so and bring help?' I pulled my sleeve back to expose the wrist band.

'Your condition makes it hard for me to fulfill my duties. I will escort you to safety.' She gripped my arm and proceeded to walk me back along the corridor. I constantly looked behind me. I was becoming concerned and felt we were being followed.

At length my fear got the better of me and I said somewhat nervously, 'Stop, Amazon, we are being followed.'

Once again she pushed my back to the wall while she surveyed the situation. 'What did you see, Earthling?'

'Nothing. I just felt they were behind us.'

'Fear will do that, but senses seldom lie,' she said as she rested her hand on my shoulder in a manner to indicate that I stay silent and still. I watched her controlled cat-like movement as she pressed herself against the wall and put her ear to it. All I could hear was the beating of my heart that almost deafened me. 'Your senses speak true, Earthling, they are approaching and there is panic in their stride.'

How the hell she knew, I shall never know, but she sure had me convinced. My heart pounded as I held my tummy as though to cradle my unborn child.

She brushed her fingers over my lips, stood with her back to me and drew both her hip lasers. Two figures appeared, two guns fired, then two bodies lay lifeless. Silently she gripped my arm and again began walking back from whence I came. To the first Arenian we met, she gave orders to take me to the hospital, then she returned to her quarry. I didn't even know her name.

Jena came to me in the hospital and showed great concern. Nada assured her all was well, but Jena wanted to know why no warning had been given. She was angry.

Karl arrived and spoke with Nada. He looked at me almost

hurt and curled his arms about me. 'I was so afraid for you, Jan darling. I thought I was going to lose you and our little girl.'

'I don't think I was in any danger, Karl. The Amazon was very protective of me when she knew I was pregnant.'

Jena called to Karl and spoke with him; their expressions were very serious. Eventually they came to me and I told them I was not feeling ill, then asked why I could not get up.

'Be patient, dear,' said Jena, 'permit Nada to be the judge in these matters.'

'Jena, will you contact the Amazons and thank them for me?'

'I shall do better than that, I will go in person.'

I touched her face and thanked her. Karl stayed a little longer until Nada told him his presence was no longer appreciated while she examined me.

I was up and about the next day, then off to the restaurant. The young Arenian who served me smiled then asked for my order.

'Just a cool drink, any kind. I just like being here.'

He stood to attention, nodded and left. It seemed impossible to make conversation with them, poor little devils.

The plump coloured lady was sitting at a table in the corner. Always alone, no one spoke to her. I thanked the waiter for my drink. He left. The coloured lady's gaze caught mine and I raised my glass to her. She raised her drink to me. I indicated an empty chair at my table, she arose and joined me. I stood and offered my arm to her. 'I am Jan the Arenian.'

She accepted my greeting and answered, 'I am Sapphire the Arenian. I see you carry a child.'

'Her father's name is Karl. He is the father of all my children.'

Then I saw the beauty of her countenance. Her eyes laughed as her ebony cheeks shone, her pearl teeth flashed. She came alive. We exchanged the names and ages of our children and found pleasure in each other's company. I was to learn a great deal that day. Sapphire was now elderly, but her mother had been taken from Earth carrying the unborn Sapphire. SHE

83

HAD KEPT THE CHILD TO THE AGE OF EIGHT, WHEN THE MOTHER DIED. Sapphire was raised by the Arenians and at the age of breeding, was given an Amazon clone to carry. At that point the Amazons had claimed her and she carried no less than nineteen clones for them. She kept in contact with all of them and loved them dearly. In return for her services, her life was now her own and the Amazons saw that she wanted for nothing. I wondered if it would be like that for me one day.

We spent three hours in the restaurant, eating and talking. I really enjoyed her company, but I had to leave to keep my appointment with Nada. We arranged to meet in the restaurant the following day.

That evening Jena and I sat in my room and talked of the day. I told her about the new friend I had made. She was quick to point out that one did not upset an Amazon or their associates, but she also added that if an Amazon accepted friendship, they would give their life to maintain it. I made up my mind there and then that I would respect and trust my new friend Sapphire.

'I was told by the Amazon Noramar that you actually sensed the escapees. Noramar was quite impressed.'

'Don't be fooled by that, Jena, I was so frightened that I would have sworn my own shadow was one of them.'

'Well at least you are truthful about your fears. Now I am off to bed and I suggest you do the same. Good night, my dear.'

I kissed her cheek and she left. I lay in bed wondering why the Amazons were so much more aggressive than the Arenians; after all, they were of the same blood. I must ask Jena tomorrow.

Next day a beautiful broad smile greeted me as I entered the restaurant. Sapphire patted a chair next to her and a waiter seated me, then awaited my order. She dismissed the waiter and pointed to a cool drink she had already ordered for me.

'It is only orange, it will feed your baby,' she told me. Afterwards we walked for a while, then we agreed to see each other's worlds. I told her I was governed by Jena whom I looked upon as a mother. Being so young it seemed to me that every one was my boss, but nice bosses. Sapphire told me that in spite of her age, she could still remember being treated the same.

'Doesn't seem fair at the time though, does it, Sapphire?'

She patted my arm and laughed heartily, 'No, child, it doesn't, but only we know they cannot do without us.'

'Come on, Sapphire, I'll show you where I'm staying.'

We took a leisurely walk back to my apartment. Jena was about to leave as I entered, so I introduced her to Sapphire. I was pleasantly surprised to see them greet each other like old friends. Jena inquired about Sapphire's girls. Sapphire spoke of them with pride. As Jena left, she told the older woman what time I had to be at the hospital and would she make it her duty to see that I was not late. Sapphire assured her that all would be well, then Jena left.

'Does Jena still work with Nada and Sadu?' asked Sapphire.

'Yes, but Sadu has been replaced by Quil. Sadu died while trying to protect me from Earth men who broke into my apartment. I also lost a child I was carrying at the time.'

Her eyes saddened as she said so sincerely, 'You are most fortunate to have Jena as a guardian. She and Nada delivered all my girls. She is one of the kindest Arenians I have ever met. Learn to appreciate what you have, child, and always return kind for kind.'

I looked into those rich dark eyes that shone with wisdom and nodded. 'Now you know why I call her Mum.'

Her teeth flashed into a grin. To make sure I wasn't late for my appointment, she took me to hospital herself and we agreed to meet the following day to see some of her family.

This time I got to the restaurant first and ordered the drinks. I asked the waiter if he wished to join us when my friend arrived.

'Thank you, Ma'am, but it is frowned upon. I thank you for your offer.'

Sapphire arrived and I told her the waiter was not permitted to join us.

'Honey, they are mighty strict with the young ones. I think sometimes they are afraid to breathe.'

'Poor little devils, they seem like nice kids.'

We drank up and went to see some of her family. She told me she was staying on the level below me and that the rooms were all the same, so she decided to take me to one of the control rooms where Amazons worked.

'Tell me, Sapphire, why are the Amazons so much more aggressive than the Arenians?'

'If you live a life of aggression, then you play aggressively. My children live for today, there is no tomorrow for them. It used to worry me, but one becomes accustomed to a way of life. You will see, child, they work hard and play hard. Fear is an unknown commodity.'

'Do they love you as their mum?'

'Bless you, child, of course they do.'

She hammered her fist on a door. It slid open, revealing four Amazons watching vision viewers.

'Hello, Mater Sapphire, have you come to check on your subordinates?'

'I brought this little one to see you, girls. I want her to know how safe Arena is with you to guard her.'

They stared at me until I wanted to dig a hole and crawl into it.

'I'm Jan the Arenian. I'm pleased to meet any friend of Sapphire's.'

'It speaks,' said one of them.

'It is with child,' said another.

'*It* has a name,' I said to them. '*It* is Jan.'

Sapphire began to laugh. 'Good for you, child.' Then she said to the Amazons, 'Now use her name and treat her like a sister, or I'll have your gut and string it round the walls.'

'Go on, Mater, thrash them,' said an older Amazon.

'Do you?' I said to Sapphire with a grin.

'Do I what, thrash them? No, I cannot catch the devils, or I might.'

I couldn't help laugh with her and the Amazons seemed to accept me.

'Is the Arenian Twenty Seven your guardian?' asked one of them.

'Yes,' I replied.

'She came to thank Noramar for taking care of you.'

'Jena told me she would thank you in person. Now I can thank you too. Tell Noramar I am very grateful to her. She was really fast with her hip lasers, it was all over before I realised it had started.'

They looked at each other, then a younger Amazon said, 'I should not talk of it to Noramar if I were you. She was angry at you for depriving her of her sport. Her kill had to be quick because of you.'

I searched their eyes, not understanding why they should want to prolong a person's suffering. I looked at Sapphire for the answer. I didn't have to ask, she volunteered the information. 'If you live and hunt like a cat, then you inherit the traits of a cat. One becomes addicted and does not want the chase to end.'

Much to my surprise, I could almost identify with that. It was not unlike a fox or a deer hunt on Earth. Or a bullfight, for that matter. Man hadn't really changed in all his time on Earth. We remained the animal. So I did not question, I took the Amazons for who and what they were, no different from anyone else on Earth.

When Sapphire saw me safely to the hospital, I did something I was not proud of. I took the coward's way of breaking our friendship. I lied and told her my holiday was cut short. I could not meet her again. Sapphire was a warm, kindly soul, but her children could never measure up to her. I would rather walk alone.

I told Jena that evening. She looked steadily at me and said, 'You always choose to learn the hard way, Jan. You only succeed in hurting yourself. Accept it as a lesson well learned. Life is not easy, my dear. No doubt there will be more tribulations in the years to come, but you will conquer them, of that I am sure.'

I went to bed with a heavy heart, a sadness I deserved for lying.

I was so pleased the holiday was over and I had returned home. One of the first things I did was to ask Jena to send a message to Sapphire wishing her and her family well and thanking her for her kindness. Jena agreed, telling me that she hoped it would help to relieve the guilt I felt. She was right as always; I felt better.

My days were busy with tests, examinations and exercising, but my evenings were full of the pleasure of being in Karl's company. Sadly our lovemaking was at an end, but being near him and seeing his smile was almost compensation enough.

It was eight thirty one evening. Karl had left and it was the time Jena and I had our last drink before retiring. Jena asked what had upset me and caused me to break my friendship with Sapphire, knowing her to be a gentle and caring person. I told Jena I was afraid of the Amazons, or at least, their outlook on life. I also told Jena of the kindly things Sapphire had said about her. I realised as I spoke of Sapphire to Jena that the lady had not only taught me a lot, but had confirmed things I already knew but had taken for granted: Jena's kindness, for example. I had given her such a hard time in my past lives and she had got me out of many bad moments, such as the time Falo seemed to be picking on me. Just like a mum on Earth, so Jena was a mum to me on Arena. I glanced at her over my cup and said, 'I'm glad I met Sapphire with all her wisdom. She reminded me of something I forgot to tell you.'

'Really, and what might that be?'

'To say thank you for being you.'

'Oh. Well drink up and go to bed,' was all she said.

I kissed her cheek, said goodnight and as I entered my bedroom I called, 'Love you, Mum.'

'I know.' Then her voice fell silent. I knew I had a mum and a friend in the next room. I was so lucky.

One more month to go for the little one to make her entrance into this world I had come to accept as home. I never asked to see any of my children now, there was too much hurt for them and me. To leave April crying and fighting her tutor or guardian was more than either of us could bear, so I left well alone. I didn't even ask Karl about them. He must have thought I was heartless.

Jena had again taken to sharing her quarters with me for an hour or so on occasions. We looked at her holiday tracks or she played her guitar to me. If I was lucky, she showed me how her computers worked and her picture log recorder. That was the cleverest computer of them all. She actually made it work one day with a picture of Karl and me sitting on the settee and got it to print it out. So I had a photo of us both at the side of my bed. Clever little devils, these Arenians.

'Jan, go into my sitting room and bring my nail cutters for me. I have broken a finger nail. Dinner will be served on your return.'

Off I went to find them. How I wished I hadn't! I opened a cupboard and staring at me were three dummy heads with wigs on them, an assortment of little glass boxes with teeth, eye glasses, lenses and tubes of paste or some such stuff.

Bloody hell, I thought: Jena's a robot! I grabbed a small pair of scissors off the shelf, quickly shut the door and hurried back to the dinner table, leaving the scissors by Jena's plate.

'Oh, you did not find the cutters then?'

I pointed to the scissors but said nothing. I didn't even look at her. We sat quietly eating. I was picking at my food more than I was eating it.

'Is everything all right, Jan?'

I just nodded.

She rested her knife and fork, then attempted to touch my hand as she said, 'Eat your dinner for the baby's sake.'

I drew my hand away, picked up my dinner and placed it uneaten by the serving hatch. Then I sat in an armchair. The silence had an uneasiness about it, almost unforgiving. She cleared the table and went to her office. I relaxed a little.

'Jan,' came her call.

'What?' I answered but did not move.

'Come here, dear.'

Sod that for a game, I wasn't going in there any more. I

didn't like robots that much. Eventually she came to the door of her office and said, 'I called you to enter. Are you coming in?'

'No.'

She entered the room and sat herself on the settee. 'You took the scissors from my vanity cupboard. I have never shown it to you because everyone has something personal which they like to keep private. Have I hurt you by not telling you?'

I slowly raised my head and met her gaze. I felt the tears welling up in my eyes. 'You let me love you and treat you like my mum, but you're not real.'

She attempted to comfort me, but realised I was ready to back away from her, so she kept her distance. 'What do you mean, dear, not real? What has happened?'

'You're a bloody robot and all this time I thought you were real.'

She sat wide-eyed with surprise. 'My dear child, I did not anticipate your fear at seeing such things. Surely you do not think I would deceive you. I am an elderly Arenian who is vain enough to want to look her best. At my age, Jan, there are very few Arenians that have not had a transplant to keep them in active health. Only a short while ago I had a new hip replaced. A robot indeed, what will you think of next?'

She held her arms open as I went on my knees and wept. She hugged my head in her lap and rocked me like a baby. Suddenly she said, 'As much as I love you, child, my hip will not take this kind of treatment.'

Together we arose, trying to help each other. With her arm about me she told me with a sly grin that I had only seen half of her wigs, there were three more away being cleaned and styled. I was full of remorse, but she only laughed at me. I also got a fresh hot meal to replace the one I had left.

'You must feed the little one,' she told me. 'Have you a name for her yet?'

'Breeze,' I told her.

'Breeze. That is most unusual. Yes, I like that name.'

Breeze was born three weeks later, although Jena said she came like a hurricane, in a great hurry. My little Breeze had arrived.

CHAPTER TEN
STAMPEDE

There was a solitude about the apartment now. In spite of Jena's company (and Mother alone knew she tried hard to be a companion to me), there was something lost that hurt me. Nada and Quil had no reason to visit. The hospital room was closed. My little Breeze had gone to her Arenian guardian. Now I felt lost and alone.

'When can Karl visit me, Jena?'

'Karl is only staying away, Jan, because it is too soon for you to mate. I know what you are going to say, Jan, but you are too persistent in your adoration. You lack self discipline. You will have to be patient and wait.'

'Oh sod!'

'Jan, let us not revert to that ungainly idiom. It is most unbecoming for a young lady.'

She was right, so I went into the garden and told all my problems to my oak tree. It couldn't repeat my swear words to anyone and I did swear amidst my tears.

I wandered back into my living room where Jena met me.

'Come, Jan, I have something to show you.'

I was fed up so I followed her, if only to kill time. She sat at her computer that filmed the living room, then placed her finger on the screen. Not only did it move into my bedroom, but beyond and into my garden. I stood silent, feeling cheated and betrayed.

'I did not put the sound up while you were out there, Jan, but I had a very good idea what was being said. What does concern me is your distress. I have no wish to see you so tearful. Perhaps I can help.'

I hung my head to hide my watering eyes.

'If I ask Karl to visit, will you promise to behave?'

'If I give you my word, Jena, I will never let you down.'

'Very well, my dear, Karl will be having dinner with us this evening.'

Suddenly I became alive.

Dinner that evening was our favourite, kidney and mushrooms. The company was my favourite, my husband and my mum. It went very well, and my longing was kept in check as I settled for second best, to curl into his arms and know that love was but a whisper away.

Jena suggested I had a break from the apartment and asked Karl to take me on a day trip. I told her I had no liking for the surface of Arena, but she brushed it aside as nonsense. It was arranged for Karl to collect me in two days' time, which would also give her time to arrange for the workers to come to the apartment to do some work that was required. I was given no choice. Never mind, I thought, I can be with Karl.

The morning arrived. Jena told me I would not need a packed lunch, it was always provided. Then the bad news came through. In Karl's sector, no one was permitted to leave their apartment due to a rock fall. He was quite safe and sent his apologies. I asked to stay home, but Jena had already made her plans and ordered a guard to escort me to the surface where she would have arrangements made for me. I wasn't happy.

As the guard reached the surface, he handed me over to a man who seemed to be organising the various trips.

'Oh yes, your guardian has contacted me. I have just the thing lined up for you. The Amazon over there is quite alone. I think she will be excellent company for you.'

I looked at the long streak of walking brawn and swallowed hard.

'I'm not really keen on a trip today, sir.'

'Have you ever been on a herding drive?'

My heart came up into my throat and my eyes almost left their sockets at the thought of being involved again with robots and a stampede. Unfortunately, he read my expression wrong. He saw surprise and not fear.

'There you are, I told you I had just the thing for you.'

He took my arm and led me to a glass-covered vehicle with dust flaps around it. He seated me in the front next to the driver and said, 'This little one and the Amazon are with you today, Sann. It is her first trip.'

The Amazon climbed in beside me, giving me a distasteful glance as she strapped her seat-belt on. So I fastened mine too. The driver started the engine and the vehicle rose a couple of feet in the air. I grabbed at the dashboard and held on for dear life.

'Sit back and relax, girl, you are quite safe,' he said.

I glanced behind to see the other passengers and almost wet myself when I saw all the seats had been removed and the back was full of herder robots.

'Robots!' I said with a distinct squeak in my voice. The Amazon looked at me as though I was nuts.

A man waved us to move as the vehicle glided forwards. Soon we were sailing across the rough terrain without a bump or a tremor. It was the ultimate in comfort. We drove over rocky and stony ground without a single jolt.

'We must have marvellous suspension on this car. I didn't feel us hit any of those rocks,' I told the driver.

'That is because we did not touch them. We ride on air, not wheels. Have you not been in a surf hover before?'

I stared at him and shook my head as I whispered, 'No wheels?'

'Lean back and enjoy the ride, girl. This is Arena!' He said it with such pride that I couldn't help but admire him for his beliefs in his land and the confidence he had in himself.

'What are you going to do with all those robots?' I asked him.

'When we find a herd we will place them behind it and let the robots drive it back,' he replied.

'I have seen a drive. I was caught up in one some time back.'

He looked hard at me and asked my name. I told him. He rested his hand on my shoulder and said gently, 'The herder masters still talk of the Earthling who almost died that day. But not today child, you are in good company.'

The Amazon turned to me and said, 'You were an escapee?'

I glanced at her but did not answer her.

After a goodly distance in the surfer, we encountered the herd. The driver said it was a herd of wildebeest. Much to my surprise, zebra also still inhabited the Earth. I felt sad that anything resembling a horse should die. I had a fondness for horses and dogs.

He stopped the vehicle to the side of the streaming column of beasts, opened the back and asked us to help him put the robots in a line leading from the front of the surfer.

'How will they know which way to drive the herd?' I asked.

'There is a compass like a homing device built in them,' he told me. He seemed quite pleased with himself for being able to answer all my questions.

He and the Amazon carried their robots, I dragged mine. Eventually we had them strung out in a line and I watched and waited for them to move.

'That low tree over there,' he pointed. 'Wait there while I bring the control switch and you will see a sight not many people have witnessed.'

He was really set to impress us. He returned from the surfer, control in hand, and pressed it while only halfway back to the tree. The robots came to life and headed towards the milling herd, who at once took flight and stampeded in a crazed circle, not knowing where to run. The driver was mesmerized by the beasts until he realised there was no set pattern to their flight. He ran hell for leather at the tree, telling us to climb as he ran. The Amazon sprang up onto a low bough and pulled me up after her. The driver followed in hot pursuit as we made our way to the crutch of the next bough, and not too soon. The beasts, crazed with fear, had panicked. They ran under the bough that we had first climbed on, snorting and leaping. Some actually hit it with their horns. At one point a robot was hooked on their horns, only to fall and become mangled under their hooves. It was impossible to see all that was going on because of the dust cloud and the fear of falling from the tree. I don't know if I was trembling with fear or if it was the vibration of the stampede. Holding tight was our main concern.

The thunder of hooves slowly died, as did the bellows of panic-stricken beasts, the smell of their sweat and the dust cloud, but it was not silent. The surf hover had been trampled and smashed. Three wildebeests lay nearby, one twisted in the wreckage of the surfer. One of them near the surfer kept trying to stand on broken legs; its grunting moans were sickening. Broken robots were scattered about and as we neared them, their sensors were triggered. They flayed their arms and kicked their legs as though running a race but going nowhere. We looked at the surfer, numb with disbelief. We were stranded in the wilderness.

The Amazon told the driver to collect all the food, water and weapons from the surfer. He clambered about the vehicle and returned with three helmets.

'There aren't any,' he said to the angry Amazon.

'Have you been doing this work long?' she asked him.

He raised his arms and let them fall to his sides before he answered, 'This is my first time.'

'It shows,' she said angrily. 'If you are as brave as you are irresponsible, there may be a slight chance that we will survive this.'

He said nothing as he passed the helmets to us. At least we had dark glasses attached to them to shield our eyes from the blinding glare of the sun.

We began to walk away from the carnage. I stopped and told him we had come from our right, but he explained we had not travelled in a straight line in order to bypass the old city.

'City? What city are you talking about? Do you mean there are people like us living here?'

'No,' he said with despair in his voice. 'They are remains of the cities. The people are called Mortorites, or murderers, take your pick. Either way, they will kill us if they can.'

We stood for a moment looking at each other. The Amazon broke the silence by saying, 'If we do not find water soon, the vultures will be feeding on us.'

I followed her gaze and sure enough, they were circling over the carcasses.

'Let's get out of here,' I said, looking back and hoping that poor beast was dead before they'd started eating it. Oh Jesus and Mother of Arena, please help us, I prayed

'I will find us water,' said the driver as we plodded on.

We must have walked for four hours. The sun was past its zenith and the driver was taking the lead with the Amazon behind him. I followed in the rear.

'Shrubs ahead,' said the driver and he quickened his pace. The Amazon turned to wait for me.

'Has he found water?' I asked her.

'If he has it will be the only thing he has done right,' she replied.

'It isn't like Arenians to foul up like this,' I told her.

'Every race has its share of idiots,' was all she said.

The driver began to run in the direction of the shrubs. Perhaps he could smell the sweetness of water or the fresh sweetness of new foliage. We all had a powerful thirst on us and the thought of a clear running stream brought new life to my stride. I would lie and immerse myself in it. What a beautiful thought!

The driver sank to his knees as though scooping the water up with his hands, then he turned to us and shouted, 'Water! I told you I would find it for you.' He was smiling at us with his success at last.

Then came an almighty splash as a crocodile's jaws closed about him and with a terrible scream from him, it turned its body as it took him through the air to the centre of the water-hole. His screams were deadened by the splashing water as other crocodiles fought for their share of him. I stood rigid, clutching the sleeve of the Amazon's jacket. Neither of us moved until the great beasts slowly sank, leaving not a ripple to indicate there had ever been anything there.

The Amazon had to forcibly straighten each of my fingers to make me let go of her, then she held my shoulders and shook me as she said firmly, 'We cannot stay here, Earthling, we must keep moving.'

She walked from the water-hole clutching my wrist, ensuring I followed her.

Night fell. I thought I would be glad of the coolness, but it was so cold. It would have been easier to walk by night, but too dangerous where poisonous creatures were concerned. We sat and huddled together for warmth.

'What's your thought on this lot, Amazon?'

'I think tomorrow will be our longest day. Perhaps our last day. We are rapidly dehydrating. What is your view, Earthling?'

'I just wish I'd never got out of bed this morning. Thanks be to the power, we don't get too many days like this.'

'Your name is Jan, yes? I am Jillard. Welcome to Arena. Do not judge all Arenians to be like our unfortunate driver.'

I looked at her and smiled, only to be reminded of the cracks appearing on my lips. She asked me why I had run away. I told her it was the only way I could prove to my elders my intent to leave Arena. After all, one cannot run to another time. She asked if I still preferred my Earth and was quite surprised when I told her Earth in my time was a thing of wondrous beauty that all Earthians must miss.

In spite of the cold, our eyes and limbs grew heavy and we slumped into slumber.

She awakened me and suggested we move again. The sun would be up in fifteen minutes. I followed her through the waist-high mist that covered the land. It drifted like cotton wool and swirled about us as we moved. Above it the land was crystal clear, but we were not alone.

'Down, Jill, get down!'

We sank beneath the haze as she turned to face me.

'I saw five heads above the mist to our right. Probably Stone men. I have been a trooper, I know I am right, Jillard.'

'The sun will free the land of this mist within thirty minutes or less. Find a depression and crawl into it. Camouflage is all we have to save us, Jan. Now stay low and dig!'

I didn't need telling twice. We scraped the ground with our bare hands, sinking lower and lower to the ground as the mist thinned beneath the rising sun. As we lay in our shallow graves it became apparent that our helmets had to be discarded because they cut an outline on the land. We half buried them, then lay in our hollow and scraped the dusty soil over ourselves. Jillard slipped her hand over mine and whispered, 'Do not be tempted to look, let the ground talk to you.' We fell silent.

I don't know about talking to me, it was living with me. I felt I was crawling with ants and wriggly things. In spite of the heat that was building up, I felt clammy and realised I was sweating with fear. How in the name of all that is holy had this situation come about? Oh, dear God!

Let the ground talk to me, she had said. Now I knew what she meant. I could hear the thud of the Stonies' tread, the faint sound of their chatter. They were here. I felt I was going to faint with the clammy heat that pressed in on me. I wanted to scream and break free. Just listen, I told myself repeatedly, just listen. Amidst the dull thud of feet came a distinct tapping, closer and closer. A snorting grunt, an investigating nudge. Then a high-pitched squeal as the investigator ran for its life and the thud of human pursuers. I could see it in my mind's eye. The Stonies were after a wild hog. Hopefully, only the hog's nose had found us.

The sounds distanced themselves from us until the only thumping I heard was the pounding of my heart. Slowly I relaxed and let my body become one with the earth. There I waited for Jillard to tell me it was safe to move.

An age passed before I heard her whisper, 'Stay while I check the land.' I waited and finally she told me all was well. We sat in our shallow grave trying to dust ourselves off.

'You look filthy, Jillard.'

'It is as well you do not have a mirror, or you would die of fright,' she told me.

We had survived. I could bear the discomfort, it was a small price to pay. We continued our trek towards a mound of rocks, crossing the path the Stone men had taken. The rock might afford us better cover. Little did we realise that the rocks were the collapsed city: the city of the Mortorites.

CHAPTER ELEVEN
MORTORITE CITY

We reached the rock and rested. I took off my helmet, wiped my brow on my sleeve and tried to rub my fingers in my hair, thinking to cool my scalp. Only dirt fell from me, so I replaced the helmet to use the visor to shield my eyes again. I didn't think it was possible to go any further, my vision was blurring. I thought I might faint, so I stayed seated.

'If you feel well enough to go on, Jillard, then do so without me.'

'We stay together, Jan, but we will rest for now.'

The rocks were sharp and not well worn like stones. I sat and examined them.

'Jillard, look!'

'Look at what?'

'We are in a lot of trouble. These rocks are man-made, they are concrete. We are in the city.'

She scanned the horizon then checked the rock. She looked me straight in the eyes and said, 'Everyone has a time to die, this is as good a place as any.'

I half smiled at her and said, 'I am tired, I'll choose my own time to sleep.'

I seemed to fumble among the sharp rocks until I was unable to keep upright any longer. I curled into a ball and felt contented with my lot. I remember trying to feel my lips. I think I fell asleep or fainted, I don't know.

Someone was holding my head under water, I could feel it seeping into my mouth, I was drowning. Then I came to, shivering with the cold as Jillard cupped my head and dampened my brow.

'Drink, Jan, it is water.' She let it run from her fingers onto my lips. Life, I felt it returning. I couldn't stop shaking with the cold, but after I had drunk and Jillard was satisfied I was out of danger, she sat me up and vigorously rubbed my back, arms and legs. The cold stiffness left my limbs and I was back in the land of the living.

'The water, Jillard, where did you find it?' I asked as I dipped my finger in her helmet and let it drip on to my lips.

'The ground told me, Jan. There is water seeping from rock everywhere, even enough to wash with,' she said with exuberance in her voice and manner.

'Well someone slipped up badly on this trip, but they sure knew what they were doing when they partnered you with me. You are a regular life-saver! Bless you, Jillard.'

'Come, Jan, let us use the moon to light our way. I will lead you to the liquid treasure.'

I followed her lead as we picked our way over and around the jagged concrete.

'Listen,' she said as she pressed her ear to the rocks. 'Listen, Jan.'

I did as she asked and sure enough I could hear the trickle of water, but from where?

'Yes, I hear it, but where? Go, Jillard, take me to it.'

It was a dirty place, full of dust. It had been a dwelling place, but only Mother knew when. The water trickled from a hole in the wall about five feet up. The wall below it had a green line with algae growing from the constant dampness. I held my hands under the gentle cascade and grinned at my prize, sipping it sparingly as though it was nectar. Water, the difference between life and death. I had taken it all for granted back on Earth.

We waited for daylight before making plans, then I celebrated my good fortune. I stripped off and began the pleasure of bathing under the small stream. It took an age, especially getting my hair clean. It was like mud. Jillard beat my clothing against the rocks to clean them and oh boy, it was pleasurable to be reasonably clean and fresh again!

Now it was Jillard's turn. As I beat her clothing, she let her plaited hair unfold. I had never seen such long hair, she was

100

going to have a mammoth task washing it, so I left her to it while I surveyed our surroundings. There were tunnels leading in all directions. Some were blocked by rock falls, a pretty dangerous place in all.

Jillard was finished and plaiting her damp hair when I returned.

'Do you feel as good as I do?' I asked her.

'Even better if we had somewhere to go,' she answered.

She was right. None of these tunnels were going to lead into Arena and two helmets full of water wouldn't get us home. We sat for a while contemplating our next move. Then I realised how hungry I was. I glanced at Jillard as I held my rumbling tummy and said with half a grin, 'You Amazons are not cannibals, are you?'

'Certainly not!' she said indignantly.

'Amen to that, because if you are as hungry as I am, then I would be mincemeat.'

'We will have to do something about that. Have you ever eaten snake, Jan?'

'Ha ha, very funny. We haven't even got a knife to kill and skin one.'

'A rock will kill it, a sharp rock will cut it. We can eat snake and survive, Jan.'

'No thanks, I like my meat cooked.'

'Then you will die. Such a waste when we have come this far.'

I looked questioningly at her and said, 'Death doesn't frighten you, does it?'

'To die in battle is honourable. To die because one does not like the taste of something is futile. I hope to die with honour, if die I must.'

'You Amazons worry me. You are so bloody conscientious in everything you do.'

'I am pleased that I worry you, it will help to keep us both alive.' She sat back and took pleasure in my dilemma. I pondered on my predicament. I must have looked mighty concerned because Jillard asked me what was wrong. I didn't bother to look up when I told her my guardian would be pacing the floor worrying about my safety.

'Did you worry about your guardian's feelings when you ran away?'

I looked at her with anger and shouted, 'That was two lifetimes ago. I have grown to love and respect her, something you Amazons have yet to learn.'

She kept silent, but her stare drove deep into me like daggers. I picked up a stone and threw it hard against the wall, then I got up and wandered into a tunnel. She followed me and said, 'It is time we moved on.'

'Well, you do whatever you want to, but count me out of it. I'm not ready to die yet, I've got someone waiting for me, so you go!'

She threw herself at me, cupped her hand over my mouth as she held me against the wall. 'Quiet!' she whispered. Slowly she released me. I was afraid to breathe for fear of a pebble falling. Voices came from one of the tunnels. Three filthy, smelly-looking individuals appeared and halted in amazement when they saw us. You could have heard a pin drop in the silence that lasted not more than five seconds. Then all hell broke loose as they rushed at us and the Amazon fought two of them and I struggled with the third. One of them pulled a gun and Jillard stood steady against the wall. Such a pity, she had been doing well. I pushed at the man holding me and moved to Jillard's side. The one with the gun approached and as he neared the Amazon he raised the gun to strike her with it. He had only been watching her, that was his mistake. I booted him in the crutch and Jillard grabbed the gun as he dropped. It wasn't a laser gun but a short rifle. How many bullets it held was anyone's guess. My worry was that it might only hold one and both the other men were armed.

'Don't shoot, Jill!' I shouted. 'Don't kill him, they don't mean us any harm.' I was standing near her with my hands up in a surrender gesture. *Don't shoot*, I mouthed once my back was to them. She held her fire.

Turning to face them, I told them we were lost. I even

helped the man up off the floor. They didn't quite know what to make of it all, then they beckoned us to follow them. The man I had kicked and helped up actually put his hand out for his gun back. A fat chance he had of that!

We followed them through tunnels all with slimy wet walls. No shortage of water here, but very dark in places. We couldn't have been too far underground because every now and then a shaft of sunlight lit the place. Eventually the men stopped and one shouted, 'Thor!'

A man walked in dressed in black leather trousers and battle blouse. He had a knife in a sheath hanging from his belt and a heavy looking gun on the other hip. His boots looked more serviceable than those his men were wearing. He stood still in the shadows.

'What is this then?' he called.

'Women, Thor. Two women.'

He moved forward into the light. There was something about him, but due to the movement of the men I couldn't think too long on it. I watched them.

'Who brought who? Don't tell me you stupid bastards let the women get the better of you?'

The voice. I knew it. It belonged to Robert the deserter. The two men with their guns still holstered said, 'We got our guns, Thor.'

The third man at this point looked afraid of Thor and to make amends grabbed at the Amazon to fight for possession of the gun she held. One shot rang out followed by *click click*. It only had one bullet.

'Leave her alone. Robert, make them leave her alone, you wouldn't let them do this to Copper ...'

A shot rang out and the man fell, holding his leg and bellowing that he was dying. Robert grabbed me by the throat and asked me who I was and what did I know about Copper. I thought he was going to choke me as I gasped and told him I was Jan the trooper. This had no effect on him and I continued to tell him I had helped him to cut off Peter the Earth man's head.

Slowly he slackened his grip as he asked in a gentler tone what had happened to Copper. I could only tell him she had been recalled from the field for breeding; beyond that, I knew nothing. He looked at me, but his gaze seemed miles away.

'I have had children, Robert, and died twice. This body you see before you is Claire, my host. No doubt she will also die in childbirth one day.'

His eyes focused again with sadness as he stroked my head. 'Forgive me. It is Jan, isn't it?'

I nodded and he beckoned me to follow him. The wounded man began shouting louder as we walked away. Robert told one of the other men to shut him up. One drew his side arm and fired. I jumped at the report of the gun and saw the wounded man fall back with a hole in his forehead. Then everyone continued walking as though nothing had happened. My eyes met Jillard's, but we kept silent.

Robert unlocked a steel door, telling us to enter, then shouted to the two men to get lost. One attempted to follow and Robert put his hand over the man's face and violently pushed him backwards, then slammed the door shut. Robert asked us to stand still in the darkness as a click was followed by a low hum that caused a dull light to appear, which grew in strength. I realised then that he had an old type generator running. He pointed to a box with a sack over it, indicating to us to be seated.

'Thirsty? he asked.

'And hungry,' I answered.

He went to the corner, picked up some tins and threw them across for us to catch. I pulled the top off of mine and saw cooked meat in it. Looking up at him I said, 'Spoon?'

'Fingers,' he replied, so I dipped in.

'Mmm, Rob, it's good, mmm lovely.'

We ate our food, licking our fingers for any morsel that might get away. As we finished, he filled the empty cans with wine. He then proceeded to tell us not to drink the water or any food offered by the Mortorites. Their main diet was rats and snakes. He also made it clear that the men only wanted us for mating and the women would kill us just for our clothing. Nice place, I thought.

Jillard kept silent, sensing Robert had little or no time for her, but she missed nothing. I asked Robert what were our chances of getting back. He reckoned getting back was not the problem, but leaving the city was. The men would want us women for themselves and would try to find a way to pass him to get us. I told him we had no way to protect ourselves. He walked across to an old chest and threw the lid back, telling us to take what we needed. My eyes almost popped out of my head. It was full of an assortment of weapons: automatic hand guns, hand bombs and knives.

'Hells bells, Robert, you've got your own arsenal here!'

'I need it with the Stone men and these cut-throats I live with.'

'Then come back with us. They will overlook everything if you get us back safe. Come back with us, Robert?' I pleaded.

He laughed heartily, telling me the Arenian dogs had taught me very little. He told me they had made him into a Thormac to do their dirty work for them. He bragged that even the Arenians were afraid of him now.

I listened bewildered to his words of hatred for Arenians, but I understood none of it.

'Choose your weapons, you will need them. And don't wear them for show or you will know the Mortorites' hatred. I don't let them have the good stuff.'

I chose a good throwing knife, as did Jillard, and Robert suggested a short-barrelled six-shot revolver. He said we could hide them better. Then he gave us a can of food each and a plastic bottle of wine as he complained the Arenians didn't even make decent drink to help you forget.

'I'll be around but I must check the wagon if I'm going to get you out of here. Don't turn your back on anyone.' Then he ushered us out and locked the iron door. We were on our own.

He left and I told Jillard that I should hate him for what he had said, but he had always treated me kindly. She was full of surprises for an Amazon; she told me that even she did not hate him. The Arenians had made him into a killing machine and it was true that they were afraid of him. His bones were reinforced with MX, a hardened plastic substance; he had an extra mechanical heart to take over from his own heart in times of stress. The higher the adrenaline the harder the pump worked and the stronger he became. He literally lived and craved danger. She said that killing him was almost impossible for one person. If she emptied all six bullets from her gun into him, he would still find strength to kill her with his bare hands and perhaps he would still not die. Thankfully he was fitted with a fail-safe in his head that could be detonated by a controller of Thormacs. It was the easiest, quickest and safest way to kill them.

I couldn't believe my ears: half man, half machine. Was it possible? Sweet Jesus, what was I doing here? I vowed I would never come to the surface of Arena again. If I made it home.

We climbed out of the tunnel through a wide crack and sat outside where we hoped we could see any attackers. There we stayed until the sun began to touch the earth to sleep the night. As we climbed back into the tunnel a flame flickered. The Mortorites had built fires and were huddling round them. They fell silent as we approached, but we hung around. Safer if you can see your foe. A man sitting round our fire was losing his hands around a woman, while a dirty little man was slowly approaching along the opposite wall, watching Jillard and me. His lusty eyes and grin said it all. Jillard slowly drew her knife enough for him to see. The grin fell from his lips and he slid back to a fire at the other end of the tunnel. My eyes met Jillard's and she replaced her knife.

The crisp crunch of boots on loose stones heralded Robert's arrival. I felt safe again. He sat himself on a rock and casually said as he met my eye, 'Well, I completed my business.' I assumed that he had transport of some kind to get us home.

'Leave her alone, Slimy. You'll have me throwing up,' said Robert to the man messing with the woman. I hung my head.

'I can make a baby,' said Slimy.

'You can't make babies any more,' said Robert grinning.

'I can, I can make babies,' insisted Slimy.

'You can't make babies without balls and you don't have any balls,' Robert told him laughing.

'What do you mean? Are they born that way here?' I asked, full of curiosity.

'He got into a fight over a woman and Sanji bit his balls off. The fool actually searched for them afterwards, so we told him Sanji ate them,' said Robert, still laughing.

'And did he?' I asked, pulling a distasteful face.

'No, but that fool believed us and he killed Sanji. So you see, Slimy, no balls, no babies.'

'But I can,' said Slimy, attempting to open his pants.

Robert drew his gun pointing it to Slimy's groin and said, 'If you get it out, I'll shoot it off.'

Slimy did his pants up begrudgingly and whispered, 'I can make babies.'

Robert stood up, still grinning at Slimy's misfortune. He beckoned me to follow him.

'What about Jillard?' I said.

'She will be all right.'

I looked at her and she indicated to me to go. He walked along the tunnel and out through the jagged crack into the cold night air. He put a friendly arm round my shoulder and told me this was what he'd missed most when he lived in Arena. He pointed to the heavens. What a night it was. The velvet sky was a mass of stars. I told him my father, a seafaring man, used to tell me about the stars, and added, 'If he was watching over me in our time, then I suppose he is in this time. All in all, Robert, we were lucky in our time. We lived in Eden and we didn't know it.'

He squeezed my shoulder and told me not to let the Arenians hear me say that. Of course he was right.

'I haven't seen too many nights like this, Robert. They were always red nights when we had to sleep out as troopers.'

'Why did you become a trooper, Jan?'

I looked about me, feeling a pained sadness and said, 'Earth men broke into my apartment. They killed an Arenian and raped me. I was heavy with child and they killed it. I wanted to kill. I wanted revenge even though the Earth men had paid with their lives.'

Robert cupped my face in his hands and drew me to him. I felt he knew my pain.

'But that's all over now, Robert,' I said looking up at him. 'Why do people hurt each other so, Robert?'

'Because we are little more than savages, Jan. For all our knowledge and understanding of life, there is an animal within us and every once in a while, we let it rule us.'

I stepped back and gazed at him. He was still holding my hand. 'I'm afraid, Robert. Afraid of you.'

He looked down at me and asked, 'How can you love your Arenian man?'

I had the feeling I knew where this was leading and I walked away from him.

'How Jan?'

I turned and faced him. 'Because he is kind, gentle and considerate. All any woman could want from a partner.'

'I could have been all those things,' he said.

'Then come back with us and find Copper.'

'I want you,' he said.

I went frigid. 'No, Robert, you want Copper!'

I hurriedly walked back into the tunnel and joined Jillard, feeling there was safety in numbers. The fires were being stoked up and their occupants were curling up on the ground around them.

'I'll show you your beds for the night,' he told us as we followed him through the iron door that he bolted behind us.

'We will leave at dawn,' he said as he threw some old sacks on the floor. 'That's the best I can do for you both.' He then pulled a box next to the gun chest and sprawled on it.

'I'll leave the light on for you, good night.'

The night closed in on us. Comfort was only a thing I longed for as I turned on the hard floor, but sleep came easy.

Suddenly I was awakened by a weight pressing down on me and as I gasped with fear, a hand went over my mouth. Jillard had woken but Robert's fist hit her jaw. 'I told you I wanted you,' he snarled at me. 'Now I'll have you!'

I turned my head to Jillard as I struggled. She was out cold. 'Don't do this, Robert, it's Copper you want.' I couldn't fight his overpowering strength, only plead with him to stop this madness. 'Copper loves you Robert, I don't. For God sake, *no!*'

I lost my fight. I felt dirty and ashamed. Where had my sense been, ever to have trusted him? I was unclean, a defiled being, unfit to mix with ethical Arenians. I got to my knees to tidy myself as Robert drank from a bottle, impervious to my predicament. I couldn't stop shaking and I was in fear of Jillard regaining consciousness and discovering what had happened. I couldn't bear the shame.

Finally I regained a little of my composure and returned to Jillard. As I attempted to raise her head, her eyes opened and her hand went to her jaw.

'Are you alright, Jill? I was worried about you.'

'What happened?'

'I moved and pushed against that piece of metal, it fell and struck you.'

I went to the corner and helped myself to a bottle, giving it to Jillard to drink. We slept no more that night and Jillard accepted my lie as the truth. Robert wouldn't take his gaze from me, it made me feel corrupt.

Morning dawned as Robert picked up a couple of bottles and told us we might need them on the way. As we left the shelter of his room the clank of the iron door wakened the Mortorites in the tunnel. They hurried towards us as one said, 'Now, Thor?'

'Tonight,' said Robert, 'wait till tonight.'

We made our way out, with the men undecided whether to follow us or not. It wasn't until we walked into a gully where Robert uncovered an old camouflaged motor that I realised our chances of getting home were at last materialising. We bundled into it and in no time at all it was revving up and rolling out of the gully. Robert stopped the car and waved to the Mortorites.

'What the hell are you doing?' I shouted at him.

'Giving them a chance to chase us in an old jaloppy. They don't have a hope of catching us, but I did promise they could have your friend.'

'You bastard, Robert!'

'Would you prefer they have you then?' he said, grinning.

'For Christ's sake, drive!'

I gripped Jillard's hand. Her face was badly swollen but her eyes were fiery. We clung to the back of the seat as he swung the car round and let it idle as he awaited the Mortorites. I punched his shoulders as I begged him not to wait, then suddenly an old open-backed car came thundering from behind.

'Race yer, boys,' whispered Robert as he put his foot down and the vehicle roared into action. We sped across the land, gradually losing our pursuers. I began to relax.

Robert slowed the car and looked behind. 'Too easy,' he said, 'let's take them through the nettle fields.'

Jillard looked fearfully at me then looked about the car. She pulled old sacking from the floor and seats, bundling them all at her feet. Obviously she was going to cushion a blow if needed, but there was no time to ask her; I had to keep track of the car coming up behind.

'Robert, go faster,' I pleaded.

The rat was enjoying every moment behind the wheel and getting twice as much pleasure from our fear in the back. Before us was a green forest. My God, I thought, I hope he doesn't go through it. If we hit a tree we've had it.

'Don't drive through the forest, Robert, we might get stuck.'

'We won't, but they will on those stingers.' There was a lust in his voice that spewed venom.

Jillard took the sacks and began wrapping them round us. I looked at her as though she was crazy.

'It is not a forest,' she said in a low tone, 'they are killer nettles to protect the entrance to Arena.'

We pulled the sacking about us as the car struck the giant

plants, cutting a path through them. As they sprang back they sprayed the car with green liquid from their crushed stems.

Robert had let the car behind come closer, and we heard screams. He wasn't content to leave it at that, he drove the car in a circle to observe the damage. The second car had stopped as its occupants beat their arms and faces in a frenzy of screaming. He opened his window as though he was immune to the poison and gloated at the men's misfortune and slow demise.

Jillard and I were dumbstruck at his audacity or just plain stupidity in leaning out of the window in such a perilous situation. The green slime slid off the roof of the vehicle, down the windows and, where there was no window, onto Robert's jacket. We watched and said nothing, but we must have had the same thought as we protected ourselves with the sacking.

Robert must have tired of watching the Mortorites. They were wild demented beings that sickened me to see and hear. He rolled the window up and with less enthusiasm he began to drive at a more leisurely pace. We watched from behind as the green liquid ran off his hair on to his neck.

'Christ,' said Robert as he tried to wipe it away, only to have the slime on his sleeve smear on to his face. In no time at all he was trying to drive and wipe his neck, face and hands. He pushed the peddle hard to the floor and began talking as he drove. 'Control, this is Thormac Nine Nine coming in with two Arenians. Help us!' he shouted. 'Help us, we are in killing nettles. *Help!*'

His driving had become erratic, and we swerved this way and that. His arms flayed as he tried to wipe at the giant blisters that were forming on his skin, only to rip and open them leaving bleeding bare flesh.

A large opening appeared in front of us and we could see the men awaiting our arrival, dressed in white spacesuits to protect them from the green poison. They parted as our vehicle raced in and spun as it pulled to a halt. Hoses were aimed at the car to wash it before we alighted, but Robert was in too much pain and couldn't wait. He clambered out as the men hosed him down. No sooner had the water washed him than the blotches of skinless burns bled.

Eventually the Arenians got Jillard and myself out. We were saturated but not burned.

'Who are you?' called a voice.

'The Amazon Jillard and Jan the Arenian,' answered Jillard.

Robert was crazed with pain. I looked at the beast of a man and slipped my hand into my clothing, bringing out the revolver. I held it tight with both hands and aimed it at Robert as I shouted, 'Payback time, Robert!'

CHAPTER TWELVE
WHISPER

The only sound I heard was the running water as I squeezed the trigger time after time. Eventually there was only the *click click* of a spent gun. People began to shout as I threw the gun to one side, then silence fell again. Robert had staggered backwards, blood covering his face, then he fell on his buttocks as his hands groped about for something to hold or support him. I drew my knife, grabbed his hair, pulled his head back and ran my knife across his throat. His airway was cut, he would not live. Pushing his head forward on to his chest I jabbed the knife into the back of his neck and up into his brain. He would kill and rape no more.

I staggered backwards into the arms of Jillard who was holding the Arenians back with her revolver as she shouted, 'No Arenian will arrest us. Only Amazons.'

I was spent of energy, but Jillard supported me and kept me on my feet until the Amazons arrived.

'They must be put in quarantine!' a man shouted.

I was lifted off my feet and taken to the quarantine facility by the Amazons. We were washed, given night clothing by the nursing staff of Arenians and left to rest under the watchful eyes of the Amazons who guarded us. They permitted no other Arenians near us. We slept like babes for twenty four hours.

We awoke with a powerful hunger and thirst. The Amazons made sure the nursing staff kept us short of nothing. My faith in mankind was returning.

An Amazon approached me, telling me my guardian Jena wished to see me. I told her I would see no one. I knew I couldn't lie to Jena and no way could I speak of what had happened; I was too ashamed.

113

After ten days in quarantine, it was decided we were well enough to face our accusers. Because the Amazons were now involved and very much in charge of the situation, we had been referred to the high court, something that frightened me.

Jillard told all that had happened accept for the time she was unconscious. Investigations were put into motion regarding the training of Sann, the driver of the surfer hover. When I was questioned, the only defence I had was to tell them of Robert's hatred for the Arenians. This was an insufficient reason for killing the Thormac.

The Arenian judge conferred with the councillors then turned to me and read the sentence. It was death by incarceration and my body was to be used as they saw fit. My brain function was to be discontinued, never to be reborn to a host.

Then all hell broke loose as Jillard claimed I belonged to the Amazons for saving her life. The female warriors encircled me, protecting me from the Arenians. As judge and Arenian councillors argued with Amazon councillors, the Amazons made it plain that they would break away from the Arenians and become a race apart. They were declaring war.

I caught a glimpse of Jena as she held my gaze. With tear-filled eyes I turned away, only to have a wall of Amazons place themselves between the Arenians and myself.

I was ushered out of the court room and taken to the quarantine hospital, not knowing what was going to become of me. I saw no one except the Amazons who guarded me and the nurses who brought me food. Jillard was back with her own kind and no news came through about the rift I had caused between Amazons and Arenians. I could only presume discussions were going on between them.

The Amazon guard entered and told me the Arenian Nada wished to speak with me on a matter of urgency. I assumed Jena might be ill, or Nada would never have become involved. I agreed to see her.

She stood just inside the door and looked hard at me.

'Is Jena ill?' I asked.

'Jena would tell you she is well, but I know differently.

Why have you refused to acknowledge her?'

I looked away from her and walked to the far wall, resting my hands on it. I stared at the floor. I had no answer for my behaviour, only my dreaded secret.

'Jan?' Nada said apprehensively. 'Jan, look at me.'

Slowly I turned to meet her eyes.

'He raped you. Oh, my dear child!'

She came to me and held me. That hug was my breaking point. I broke down and wept, begging her not to tell Jena of my shame. She asked why I had not mentioned it when the blame was not mine, and asked where Jillard had been when it happened. Then I told her of my lie about Jillard being knocked unconscious by a falling piece of iron.

Nada asked me to trust her, telling me that she would try to arrest this terrible division threatening Arena. With a promise to try to return, she left me with my shame, although in truth I felt better for having shared my secret.

Three days later, I was escorted to the courtroom. By this time I had yet another secret. Nature had told me I was pregnant. What an unholy mess to be in, carrying a child of the Devil! I prayed that its name might never be spoken aloud, for the shame I bore.

There was order and orderliness in the courtroom this time. Amazons were conspicuous but held their silence for the main part. I was told to make a true statement to avoid punishment. At this point I was past caring if I offended or pleased, and I shouted at my examiner;

'Do you think I want the world to know I killed the father of my child?'

The courtroom fell silent at my statement. I took the opportunity to scan for Jena. She gave a nod of her head, in approval, I hoped.

'The court will require a fully recorded account of the incident via a memory recorder,' said the interrogator, obviously not believing a word I was saying.

Nada rose from her seat and made her way down to the interrogator. 'The child has had no experience of a mind recorder. It could be detrimental to her peace of mind and her present state of health,' she said.

'Then let her neuro-surgeon perform the task,' ordered the man.

The case was adjourned until they had the proof they required and still I was not allowed home.

The following day I was taken to Minu's place of work where Jena, Nada and Minu's assistants Icna and Amni were awaiting me. My Amazon guard stood on sentry outside the door. I was full of remorse at having turned my back on Jena, but she was very understanding and forgiving. Her concern was for my condition.

Minu offered to show me more of his precious stone collection. I told him I had no interest in them, as pretty as they were. He turned to Jena, telling her an injection was the only alternative.

Jena explained that if I did as Minu asked, I would feel no discomfort. Reluctantly I agreed and Minu injected me as I lay in a reclining chair and a dream recorder was placed on my head. I counted backwards from ten as I felt the restrainer straps put across me. It was too late to struggle, I just wanted to sleep. Then my dreams began. Every time Minu told me to remember, I relived that terrible ordeal.

When I awoke, my energy was spent. I was allowed one hour to recuperate, then taken by the Amazons who permitted Jena to come with me back to the quarantine centre.

Jena left, informing the nurse that Minu had recommended giving me a sleeping tablet and telling her to expect me to have a restless night.

I don't know what kind of night I had; I remembered nothing. I also felt fit for nothing.

Then it was back to the courtroom in the afternoon. Perhaps today they would tell me when I must be terminated. I felt too ill to care, taking in little of my surroundings. When I was spoken to, it took an age for me to comprehend and give a sensible answer. It wasn't important any more. I stood there, I listened, I answered. People moved too quickly for me to focus on them. Then Jena said to me in her kindly way, 'Come along, dear, we are going home.'

The next thing I remembered was sitting on the settee with Jena, sipping a nice cup of tea. Then I went to bed as she sat at the side of my bed. I felt safe once more.

Morning dawned and with it a sense of perspective to my world. As I sat at the breakfast table and listened to Jena talk of mundane things, I interrupted her and asked what the outcome of the trial had been.

'You really did not comprehend anything that was said yesterday, did you?' she said.

'I don't remember anything at all,' I told her.

She replenished my cup, then gave me the good news that I had been acquitted of my crime against Arena, so quelling the uprising of the Amazons.

'When can I have my pregnancy aborted?'

'That, my dear, is the bad news. They ordered that you carry the child full term and have a normal birth. I am sorry, Jan.'

I said nothing, knowing that Jena didn't make the rules. I had to be grateful for my life, such as it was. Breakfast over, I retired to my garden to tell my oak tree all my thoughts and fears.

'I can understand why you love this garden so, it is very pretty and welcoming,' said Jena as she stretched out her hand to help me up.

'How is your hip?' I asked, afraid to accept her gesture in case I caused her pain.

'Improving by the day,' she replied, laughing.

I arose and together we walked through the garden.

'Everything looks so clean, fresh and colourful, Jena, yet I feel so dirty. Are you ashamed of me?'

She put a friendly arm round my shoulder, telling me nothing could be further from her mind. She told me she was more concerned with the scarring of my mind than that of the body. I squeezed her hand and we walked back into the living room. She suggested we have company in a day or two, but I showed no enthusiasm. She let the matter drop.

Time drifted by. I was quite contented in the apartment with only Jena's company. Nada visited a couple of times a week, not in a working capacity, but as a friend and I think as company for Jena. She was less stringent with me and acted more like Jena, like a friend.

'We have a surprise visitor for you this afternoon, Jan.'

I wasn't impressed. If it was going to be Karl, then I wouldn't be at all pleased. I dreaded having to face him with another man's child within me. I ignored the talk of visitors and retreated to my garden.

'Jan, your visitor has arrived.'

I sauntered in and got the surprise of my life. It was my sister Fern. I threw my arms round her and almost crushed her. It was wonderful to be with her again.

She stayed three hours and the time flew by. Both Fern and Jena got on well together, which pleased me greatly, then the penny dropped. Fern told me she had carried her clone. Jena and Nada had delivered it. It served to make the family bond greater.

Fern, it seemed, was a trooper. That worried me, knowing the dangers out there, and I made her promise to be extra vigilant. Not once did she mention my pregnancy; that would have embarrassed me. I so hoped she would visit again.

My wishes were acknowledged. Karl did not visit, but time was passing.

Nada and Quil made regular visits. They were worried because of my lack of appetite and weight loss. Jena sat at the table with me, our meal finished, the table cleared. She reached across the table and held my hands. 'I have been checking your log record, Jan.'

'And?' I asked, just wondering what she was getting at.

'Have you thought of a name for your little girl? Would it be Whisper?'

I tried to pull my hands away, but she held them fast.

'No, Jan. You cannot keep avoiding the inevitable. I saw what you wrote. You are hardly eating enough for yourself, most certainly not enough for both you and the child.

Whatever Nada and I give you to supplement your lack of eating can do you no good if you have not the will to fight. Do you have a death wish?'

I pulled my hands to free them, but to no avail. She intended that I face her and hear what she had to say.

'Shall I quote what I read?' she said firmly.

I turned my head away.

'Let their names drift on the Breeze,
Whisper, Echo, lost in time.
Let them share the love that you give,
Do not tell them they were mine.
How many times must I tell you, Jan? The blame was not yours.'

'Please, Jena, please let me go!'

She freed her grip, if only to let me get my handkerchief to mop my tears.

'Jan, my dear, I beg you not to do this to yourself. It is cruel, not only to the baby, but to me also. I look upon you as my child, I do not want to lose you again. Eat, my dear, if only for me.'

'There's no point if I cannot be reborn again.'

'Jan, I told you that you were exonerated. Of course you will be reborn. My dear child, I blame myself for not making the decision of the court plain to you. I had no wish to hurt you more by discussing it further.'

I wept in her arms, promising to try and help myself, even knowing that each mouthful I ate made me feel ill.

Nada and Quil came more often and Nada would stand by me while I drank special concoctions that she assured me had lots of vitamins in them. They tasted great, but I couldn't keep them down.

Two weeks before I was due to give birth, it was decided to bring the birth forward. Jena told me I was getting weaker.

'But I've tried to eat more Jena, I just can't keep it down.'

'You left it too late, Jan,' said Nada, 'but we will do all that is within our power for you, I promise.'

119

The hospital wing was prepared and Minu came with his special metal trolley. I was made ready with drips in both arms. The screen was placed to obstruct my view of the birth as I awaited my fate, be it live or die. Mother, I didn't want to die.

Jena took care of me as Nada and Quil worked to deliver the girl child. Minu was ready with the anaesthetic as he watched, intrigued by Nada and Quil's work.

'Increase the drip,' came Nada's voice.

I watched Jena for any sign, but she gave nothing away.

'We need her help, Jena.'

Jena told me to push.

'It is too weak to fight, make her bear down.'

Jena gripped my face and grunted with me as I tried to push. 'You are on your own, Nada,' she said, 'she is exhausted to the point of fainting.'

'I shall have to use the machine, the heart is weakening. Jena, be ready with the oxygen or we will lose her.'

'There she is,' said Nada, 'such a tiny little thing. Put her into the incubator, Quil.'

'What are you naming her, Jan?' asked Quil.

'Whisper,' I whispered.

'What was that?'

'Whisper,' said Jena.

'Oxygen, Jena,' rapped out Minu. Jena looked at him very seriously. 'Yes, I'm afraid so,' he said, 'she is far too weak.'

Jena continued what she was doing then nodded to Minu.

'The dark time?' I whispered.

She looked down at me as she stroked the hair back off my face and said, 'You are too weak to continue. Nada has tried hard to do the impossible. Your heart cannot take any more strain. You will go to sleep while Minu does his work. I shall be waiting for you when you awaken.'

'Will I be reborn then?'

'Yes, my dear, with long fair hair, blue eyes and fair skin. Does that meet with your approval?'

'Just be waiting for me.'

'Breath deeply. That's right.'

'I love you, Mum.'

My eyes grew heavy and as I looked into Jena's eyes, I swear they were watery. Arenians don't cry, but my mum cried for meeee...

End of Log Book Three